ENTANGLED ESSENCE

STOLEN LEGACY, BOOK TWO

CANDICE BUNDY

PIPER FOX

CONTENTS

PROLOGUE - FLOAT TANK

EMRYS

"Hello?" I called out, but no one answered.

An oppressive darkness wrapped around me, sealing me off from the world beyond. My body felt no different, but as I blinked my eyes, there was nothing to see. Nothing to touch past my skin. When I spoke, I could hear myself, but the sound was dampened, as if I was in a tiny space. The ground was flat, and the whole place felt like a mysterious blank canvas. I had yet to locate any walls.

The last thing I remembered was the fae Taneisha proclaiming me a thief before she magically transported me into this void. My word, not hers.

She was right, although I'd never admit it. She'd given us a nearly impossible task, so I figured gaming the system was expected. Next time, I'd have to be more careful.

It felt like minutes had passed. Or was it years? I knew she'd keep me here as long as it satisfied her whims. If the time matched how long she could hold a grudge, I was in serious trouble. Anything to exact more punishment for my years of perceived slights towards her back during our Academy days.

I sat down. At least it felt like I did. Palms on my forehead, I sighed in exasperation.

Taneisha flashed into existence in front of me. A nimbus of rosy light with no discernible source surrounded her. She sat down across from me, the layers of her rose petal covered skirt forming a sea of color. Her sandy hair fell in waves, framing her face. My eyes greedily drank in the sight, eager for any form of stimulation, even if it was a fae I couldn't stand.

"How's my prisoner?" she asked, arching an imperious brow.

While she had a grace and glamour few others could hope to emulate, I'd always thought of her as aloof. Too stuck up for the rest of us. Despite her beauty, there was nothing attractive about her, and I found her polished appearance repellent.

"How long do you plan to hold me here?" I asked.

I had to get out, but how, when this was yet another reality the fae had constructed? My Isis-lineage magic gave me influence over healing and insight, but so far, I was at a loss over how to strategize my way out of her enchantment.

Perhaps I could charm my way around Taneisha's grudge?

She shrugged, a slight smile inching across her face. "It depends on your posse and the mage. Once they find Caden's seeds, I'll return you to them."

"And if they don't?" I had to know. Would she keep me here forever? Could she?

Her gaze dropped, like she didn't want to admit the answer. "Let's hope they do, Emrys."

Anxiety needled through my chest. What wasn't she telling me?

"You have no right to hold me here, Taneisha. What is this place, anyway?"

"It's a penalty box. I crafted it with you in mind."

That wasn't ominous. Not at all. "It feels more like a sensory deprivation chamber," I replied. A shiver that ran down my spine. Was she just trying to make me sweat? Freak out?

"That's exactly what it is," she said, pursing her lips. "Knowing you, I figured you'd never be able to rein yourself in and follow my rules. So, I constructed this special place just for you. It's an opportunity for you to have some alone time with your thoughts."

"That's exactly what I don't need," I grumbled. I got this kind of crap from my Granny, like I needed it from a flighty fae I hadn't seen in years? I lived fast for a reason. Slowing down to meditate on my life's purpose or plan my long-term goals was something I'd happily avoid as long as possible.

"On the contrary, I think this is precisely what you need. Time and space to rethink your life. Who are you without your friends to play off of? This is an opportunity for growth."

She was brimming with hypocrisy. I couldn't let her know she'd gotten to me, so I forced out a laugh. "Yeah, cause you're the epitome of mental health."

Taneisha arched her brow. "At least I know what I want."

I wasn't sure what to make of her vampish smile, and

she was obviously trying to bait me, so I held my tongue. I didn't want to piss off my jailor. From what I'd seen so far, Taneisha would have no qualms about making my already unpleasant situation worse.

When I didn't reply, her eyes lit up. Taneisha leaned in close. "Emrys Tedros, able to keep his mouth shut? Well, I never thought I'd see the day," she whispered. "Perhaps there's room for growth after all?"

Was Taneisha flirting with me? I genuinely couldn't tell. Perhaps I could seduce her into letting me go? I considered the possibility, but my mind drifted back to Sera. A pang of sadness hit me square in the gut. I'd wanted her for myself, yet the shifters had gotten to her first. I sighed.

Taneisha patted me on the shoulder, no doubt thinking my sigh was about this situation, and not Sera.

"Do you think your friends are working hard to free you as fast as they can?"

"I'm confident they'll do what it takes to free me."

"But not necessarily as quickly as they can, right?" she teased. "I bet they'll get distracted with Sera, too. A cute, sexy, powerful mage like her. Who wouldn't want a piece of that action?"

My mind filled with images of Sera fucking Liam and Marcos while Caden and Franc watched, and I had to take a slow breath to keep from snapping back at her.

"Poor Emrys," she pouted. "It must have hurt to be excluded back there. How much more do you think you'll miss out on while you're apart from them?"

Taneisha appeared intent on baiting me, and it was clear she knew what had happened between the group in Golden. Worse, she was right. It had hurt to be excluded, especially when I was the one who'd brought Sera along on the ride with our posse. Not that I wanted to share her with any of them, and the exclusion felt even more profound for it.

What would happen while I was away? Would I come back to find them all settled into some sort of quasi-relationship? Worse, what if they didn't forgive me for breaking Taneisha's rules and leaving them one down for solving Caden's quest?

"You saw the marks on Sera's back?" I asked, and she gave me a knowing nod. "Did you do that?"

She shook her head. "I can't claim credit for those mating marks, but boy, what a doozy of a reveal it was for you guys."

"I'm not inclined to believe you. I mean, they showed up right after we crossed into faery. Surely the two events are related."

"Fae magic can have weird effects when it crosses the magic of other supes," Taneisha explained. "Sometimes things speed up or reverse in action. We're mercurial."

Why not take credit if she could? I frowned at her, tempted to believe her. Taneisha had engineered all of this just for us and seemed damned proud of herself. "You're saying your fae magic might have sparked something already there, under the surface?"

"Maybe?" she shrugged. "Too bad you're stuck here while everyone else is figuring it out, huh?"

"If you're so worried about me, you could send me back."

"I'd never dream of depriving you of your experience. If you need anything, just say my name out loud," she said with a wink, and then stood up and smoothed her skirts.

"I'd be happy to sit with you as often as you'd like as you wait for your friends to bail out your inappropriate behavior."

"I'll keep that in mind." I swore right then that I wouldn't call her name. This fae would not get the best of me.

"Ta-ta for now, golden boy," Taneisha said, and then disappeared out of existence.

She left me in the darkness, and I settled in for a long wait. I repeated a mantra to myself, over and over.

I can manage this. I'll survive.

I have to.

MOUNTAIN OF MYSTERY

I ran a hand through my hair, pulling it off my neck to cool my skin, wishing I'd remembered a hair tie. We trudged along under the moonlight, every step a weary challenge. Going back and forth through faery meant shifts in time, so I wasn't clear how many actual hours, or even days, had elapsed since we'd started this journey. However, it was evening when we first travelled into faery and then we'd spent half a day getting the Eye of the Tiger. It was safe to say we were all running on fumes.

The trail we were on skirted around the base of the mountain, slowly gaining in elevation as we went. Despite the moonlight, it was fairly difficult to see the path before us, and I kept snagging my feet and stumbling. After my third or fourth misstep, Marcos scooped me up, cradling me in his arms as he walked.

"This can't be safe," I said. "If you trip, we'll both fall."

"You're exhausted. Plus, my night vision is much better than yours," he rumbled. "I won't go down."

"That's not what you said earlier," Liam said.

I smirked, remembering the intimacy we'd shared back in the shed at the pixie habitat center, but then a shyness crept in. What had happened between all of us was hot and fantastic and I didn't regret a moment of it. I'd even played the instigator, but I wondered what the guys thought of that. None of them at the time had seemed to mind me being so forward and demanding, but there hadn't been a lot of discussion since.

When Marcos didn't respond to Liam's jibe, my anxiety eased somewhat. I laced my arm around Marcos' neck, taking comfort in his calm strength.

Taneisha had made it clear the hunt for Caden's jar of seeds wouldn't be as easy for us as the last round. The rules were the same. One chance to win back the item. No cheating. No stealing. Now here we were, in a forest, at night, with some thief to face off against after we reached our destination at the top of the mountain. Who knew what else awaited us along the way?

"Do you know where we are, Caden?" I called back over Marcos' shoulder. I could barely make him out behind us, but I knew it was Caden because his eyes flashed demonically red in the moonlight.

There was a pause before he answered. "I think I do. This mountain is familiar. The smell of the air is too. But I can't be sure."

"But you have a guess," Liam said. "So out with it."

Caden sighed. "This place smells like a daemonic realm adjacent to our own. But we can't actually be there."

"Why not?" Franc asked. "We've been back and forth to faery twice in the last day, or however long fae time is. What's different?"

"Because only demons can travel back and forth through the veil to the Netherworld," Caden explained. "Your races can't cross over."

"What about fae? Can they cross the boundary?" I asked.

No one answered.

As much as this quest worried me, I feared Emrys had things worse back with Taneisha. He didn't strike me as the type to enjoy a lot of alone time. Plus, the hurt look on his face when he'd walked in on all of us enjoying ourselves haunted me. Now that he'd been locked away, we couldn't even talk things out.

"What do you guys think the penalty box is like?" I asked.

There was silence for a few steps. I knew they all worried about him. They had to be. Emrys could be cocky and irritating, but he was still like a brother to each of the guys.

"Whatever he faces, Emrys will persevere," Franc replied. He'd taken up the lead with Liam, scouting our path through the dim light. "He's been through worse and is more resilient than his reliance on hair pomade might lead you to believe."

"Taneisha said she'd return him after we successfully retrieve Caden's seeds, so that's what she'll do," Liam added. "None of us will risk Emrys, despite his questionable behavior, if that's what you're worried about."

"I wasn't worried," I replied. "I just figure whatever Taneisha cooked up for him will be awful."

No one speculated aloud. Perhaps they worried the fae could be listening and use our speculations as inspiration to punish Emrys?

When I heard a rustling, I looked back over Marcos' shoulder. Caden had what looked like a map out, somehow looking it over in the dark while also keeping his footing. Did demons have better night vision than me, too? Was I the only one here who couldn't see well in the dark?

"There are a series of switchbacks coming up," Caden said. "Perhaps we could stop and rest before we head up?"

"That doesn't sound wise," Marcos said. "We don't know what's out there."

"I know we're all tired. When you're tired, people can get sloppy and make mistakes," Caden replied.

"Not all of us get sloppy," Marcos snapped back. "And none of us are people."

Marcos said Caden had fallen into addiction and was potentially dealing drugs, and so I hadn't expected him to have thought out this much of a plan. Unlike most of supe society, I knew the posse didn't look down on him for being an incubus, but some did for the company he kept. I'd seen that Franc and he had an intimate relationship, so it appeared the demi-god trusted him. But there was clear friction between the shifters and Caden, friction that could cause issues on our quest.

I resolved to pay more attention and come to my own conclusions about Caden. I was the outsider in this group, so perhaps I could bring a fresh perspective. At the least, I needed to learn more of Caden's history and the item Taneisha had stolen from him.

"We have to rest sometime," Caden insisted.

"Sound logic," Liam replied, taking off his backpack.

He shucked off his clothes, stuffing them inside. When he was naked, he handed his pack over to Franc. "I'll run ahead, see if I can find any defensible areas within easy distance from the trail."

"Do you want me to come with you?" Marcos asked.

Liam caught me ogling him, and his lip curled, full of smug confidence. I shivered under the sudden intensity of his gaze. I really should have asked Taneisha about the mating marks and if her fae magic might be responsible, but there hadn't been time.

"No, stay with Sera. I'll let you know if I run into trouble." A moment later, Liam shifted into his wolf form, and then he shot off into the underbrush. I caught glimpses of his brilliant snow-white fur as he darted about in the distance.

Marcos held me tight as we continued along the path, and I couldn't help but cuddle up closer against him. He believed me to be his mate, and although I didn't feel any desire to be claimed by him, I couldn't deny secretly enjoying his drive to protect me. Especially when he'd already shown he wasn't trying to boss me around.

Who wouldn't want a big, strong shifter around to protect them? Or two? I felt heat fan my cheeks, and Marcos glanced at me.

"I'd give more than a penny for those thoughts," he whispered.

Just then, a sharp cry in the distance carried through the night air. Everyone came to a stop and waited.

"It might be nothing," Franc whispered. "Just a bird. Or a hyena?"

Another long, plaintive yowl cut him off. Not from the

same location, and it sounded nothing like an owl or enormous bird.

Why was I convinced it was responding to the first cry we'd heard? "That's not nothing," I said, squirming against Marcos to be let down. "Let me walk."

"Can I carry you so we can move faster while you watch behind us?" Marcos asked.

"Okay, fine," I said, and he took off.

"Liam says he's found a place up ahead. Let me lead," Marcos said, and the others fell into step behind us.

"That shifter telepathy skill is pretty handy," I muttered.

I watched over his shoulder, but my night vision wasn't that great. I could make out Franc's focused expression and Caden's pale skin and white around his eyes. When another yell pierced the surrounding silence, I didn't miss the look of terror on Caden's face.

"What's out there?" I asked Caden.

"I don't…" he started.

"Guess!" Franc demanded, cutting him off.

His eyes met mine, and for a moment I thought he wouldn't answer. "Ghouls."

His answer struck terror in my heart. Creatures out of legend, they were predators saved for scary stories around a campfire late at night with a bottle of wine. I'd never seen one or heard of anyone who had. Then again, my experience wasn't exactly extensive. "Wait, the undead flesh-eating kind of ghoul? Real ghouls?"

"You need to get out more often," Franc said, his breathing ragged. I doubted he ran much unless he was running late to a party.

If we were lucky, they weren't after us, but we couldn't

take that risk. There might just be a couple of lone wanderers, or there might be a pack of them. I searched the path behind us, my heart racing in my chest.

That's when I spotted the gleam of moonlight reflecting off of multiple sets of eyes in the distance.

GHOULS JUST WANNA HAVE FUN

SERA

"There's two. No, three," I called out. There was no point in being quiet when they were already onto us. The creatures were still a ways behind us, but there was no doubt they were gaining.

Somehow Marcos ran even faster despite carrying me. Franc kept up, but Caden was falling behind.

"Can't you do something magicky?" Franc yelled at me.

Could I? Sure, if they got close enough, I could zap or burn them, but not while Marcos was carrying me. I'd likely burn him, too. The chaotic spin to my magic meant I couldn't predict if it would work or what it would do, but could I leverage that now to my advantage?

"Not like this," I replied.

Coming around a curve in the trail, moonlight illuminated a river ahead of us. Beyond it, the trail banked hard up the mountain.

"Liam says the water's fairly shallow, but the bottom is slick in places, so we have to slow down," Marcos said as we reached the water's edge. I could tell his attention was divided between our conversation and the one he was holding with Liam in his head. "There's a cave ahead that Liam's checking out. It's a more defensible location than open ground."

"Let me down," I demanded, and he did without argument. I forged ahead, the icy water soaking through my shoes. Luckily, the riverbed was a similar gravelly material as the trail, so it wasn't terribly slippery, despite the water coming up to my knees.

"This is a dangerous plan," Franc replied, glancing back at the monsters.

The three men followed me across the river, but it was slow going as the river was wide and none of us wanted to fall on our faces.

"Will they follow us across the water?" Franc asked.

"No clue," Caden replied. "But let's assume, yes?"

"I feel like that's something you should know, demon. How do we kill them?" Marcos asked Caden.

"Separate them from their heads," Caden explained. "Also, don't get bitten or clawed, or you could get infected."

"Did anyone see any weapons in the bags?" Marcos asked.

"Only the folding knives," Caden replied.

"Tink had to know what she was throwing us into," Franc said, his tone full of frustration.

"She really doesn't like me," Caden replied, sounding disappointed.

"You think?" I asked.

We reached the other side of the river, and I looked back across the water. I couldn't see the beasts, but their hooting cries meant they weren't far off. "How much further to the cave?"

"It's just past the second switchback," Marcos replied.

"We need a distraction, mage," Franc said. "Something to slow them down. Please tell us you have something up your sleeve?"

I looked from Franc to Marcos, who already knew my secret. Marcos' expression was grim, but he shrugged, which I took to mean why not just try something.

What could go wrong? Like, a lot with my chaotic magic. At least here there weren't any structures around for me to destroy. While I debated my options, the beasts cries were only getting closer.

"Whatever you're going to do, do it now," Caden added.

"Head up the trail," I ordered. Franc and Caden listened, booking their way up the trail.

"I'm not leaving you alone here," Marcos said, staring down the darkness as he stood by my side.

Which was super hot. And sweet. But I knew my magic, and for all of Marcos' good intentions, I wouldn't risk him.

"Then I strongly advise you back up," I said, realizing I couldn't say anything to make the panther leave.

I walked forward to the water's edge, raising hands that erupted with mage fire as I visualized my intentions. Blazing purple fire spat and sputtered. What? Purple this time? What did that mean? Would I get lucky? Would my magic heed my command?

I brushed those thoughts aside, focusing on my will. The pressure of hearing the ghouls converging, along with the sputtering of my mage fire, rattled my nerves.

Come on, Sera. Pull it together and fire things up.

I focused on the water flowing before me, and my mage fire shot into it, inundating the liquid with billowing waves of luminescent power. The fire spread from my hands up and down the shallow river, illuminating the night with an ethereal glow. When it had stretched as far as I could see, I flicked my hands up, directing the energy upwards.

To my delight, a wall of mage fire rose from the river, surging nearly twenty feet high. I drew the sigils to lock the spell in place, and then pulled my hands away from the magic, stepping back. Despite my reservations, I'd done it! The wall churned and spat, sure, but it held.

Impossibly so, considering the historic chaotic bent to my magic.

For a moment I just stood there, wondering how it held together. My magic had a history of failing, often spectacularly, or never coming together. Why was it working now? Here? Or was it flawed, and I just didn't see how?

Perhaps this wasn't the best idea? But it looked okay, so, yay? I reached for a confidence I didn't feel.

"Nicely done," Marcos said, once again by my side. "And you doubted your powers."

"I'm not entirely sure it'll hold," I replied. "Or behave."

"I'm sure it will give them pause," Marcos replied.

"Cool trick," Franc called from up the trail. "We should still get out of here. Now!"

I wasn't arguing. I spun and headed up the trail, sprinting after Franc and Caden, Marcos at my side.

Just as we reached Caden and Franc, angry shrieks filled the night behind me. I couldn't help it; I stopped and turned to watch. Would my wall of fire hold? I saw three creatures on the other side of the river, their glowing silver eyes tinged pink through the wall of fire. They might have once been human, but their thin, naked bodies looked like husks that had been left out to dry under the desert sun. Even from this distance, I could make out their exaggerated sharp teeth and long claws.

The three ghouls were soon joined by two more. Just how many were there? They snapped their jaws and moved close to the river, caution overriding their need to pursue us, at least for now.

"How long will it hold?" Caden asked.

Great question. If only I knew? "It depends."

Franc swore under his breath. "This is not the time for the stereotypical cagey mage attitude."

"Cool it," Marcos replied, shutting Franc down. "Let's get to the cave."

I headed up the trail, my attention split between my footing and the wall of mage fire. The river was easy enough to keep an eye on, as there weren't many trees on the hillside to block our view, and the mage fire illuminated everything. We made it to the first switchback when a crackling, popping sound filled the valley.

A ghoul had entered the river, and a white-hot nimbus surrounded him as he caught fire. The fire churned and popped around him, exploding, spreading streams of mage fire sailing through the air, well beyond the banks of the shallow river. Wherever the file landed, it spread like napalm, burning, and spreading of its own accord, feeding on any flammable material in its path.

Despite the fire, the ghoul kept moving, resolutely crossing the river. When it reached the other side, it emerged as a flambeed ghoul, filled with everlasting, pink-tinged mage fire.

"Well, fuck," I whispered.

"Is that how it's supposed to work?" Franc asked.

"Nope, that's a whoops," I admitted.

"Let's keep moving," Marcos replied. We all started moving again, but we couldn't help but watch the ghouls below.

"How long will it take for the fire to destroy it?" Caden asked.

Would it end them? Mage fire destroyed almost everything. But that ghoul looked to be doing just fine.

Damn my magic!

"I'm really not sure. Mage fire will burn about anything, so I figured it would destroy them. I admit I don't have any experience with ghouls."

The ghoul who made it across hooted back at the others, who followed the first creature into the river of fire. The second ghoul, upon contact with the purple fire, exploded, sending mage fire streaming out in all directions. The other three, undeterred, rushed the river together, as if passing through it quickly might help them avoid exploding like the last one. One of them exploded, and then another. The last one passed through the barrier like the first, howling in triumph as it exited the wall of flame.

The two flaming ghouls looked each other over and then turned their ravaged faces in our direction. The wall continued to emit fiery sparks and explosions, as the dead ghouls within fed the flames. The mage fire spread, and I worried how long and how far it would burn.

"We're almost to the cave," Marcos said. I could hear Liam's wolf yipping just around the switchback.

"So now, instead of fighting ghouls, we get to fight

flaming ghouls?" Franc said. "This day just keeps getting better and better."

"At least there's only two," Marcos said.

We hit the second switchback, my legs burning with the intensity of our exertion as we pounded up the steep incline. Liam's white fur gleamed in the moonlight, a beacon calling us to the protection of the cave. When we reached him, I realized he was a good ten feet up a sheer rock face. Liam shifted, regaining human form, and reached down, offering a hand up.

Franc reached the rock wall first, offering a leg up to Caden with his hands clasped together. Caden tossed his backpack up the wall and onto the ledge, and then put his foot into Franc's hands and jumped up, reaching Liam's outstretched hand easily.

"You're next," Marcos told me.

I pulled off my backpack and tossed it up to Liam. I didn't hesitate, stepping into Franc's hands, then jumping up and grabbing both Caden's and Liam's hands. They hauled me up, and I rolled past them, needing to get out of the way. Another two backpacks landed on the rock beside me, and I pulled them away from the edge, tossing them against the cave wall. They pulled Franc up next, and I expected Marcos, but he didn't follow.

When I looked down over the edge to the trail below, a golden-eyed black panther met my gaze.

Icy panic flooded my veins. "No, you can't stay down there," I called out. "Get up here, Marcos!"

Liam was right in front of me, his hands on my shoulders. "He's a scrapper and he can handle himself. We both can."

I knew what Liam was getting at. He was about to join

Marcos and fight off the ghouls. "No, don't go. This is crazy. We can wait them out up here. The ghouls will burn up or get bored."

His tender smile touched my heart. "I won't have Marcos go this alone. We need to finish the ghouls off, or they might draw more." Liam looked at Franc and Caden. "Protect her."

Liam shifted, his wolf form still larger than I expected, and nuzzled my cheek and neck before he turned and leapt off the cliff to the trail below.

"We can't let them do this," I begged Caden and Franc. Franc came to stand next to me at the cliff edge, but Caden held back.

"I've seen both of them fight," Caden said, his brow knit with worry. "Especially Marcos. He's a beast in any form."

"I'm going to check the bags for weapons," Franc said, placing a comforting hand on my shoulder. "Be careful this close to the edge."

Franc moved to help Caden search through the packs, and I groaned in frustration. Then I caught sight of the ghouls coming around the second switchback, and my heart skipped a beat. Liam and Marcos had the high ground, but would that be enough?

As if in answer to my question, one of the remaining ghouls exploded, sending a burst of mage fire out in all directions. The remaining ghoul cowered from the blast, but then rallied, screeching into the night.

"That's some luck," Caden said, taking a couple of steps closer to the edge, no doubt looking for a view of the action after that explosion. He looked even more anxious than I felt. "Where did Marcos go?"

"I dunno, he was right next to Liam." I leaned forward, scanning the area. "I can't make out his form in the dark."

Franc's hand came around my waist, pulling me back a step from the edge. "Careful, sweet, mind the edge." He pressed a knife into my hand but kept me close. "Take this."

"The blade's only six inches long. What use would it be against that?" I asked, motioning to the flaming ghoul advancing on Liam's hunched, growling form.

"It's better than nothing," Franc whispered against my ear. "Keep quiet. We don't want to draw attention to our location."

I gave over and slumped against him, gripping the knife firmly. Franc was right, but I didn't have to like it. In the distance, my mage fire erupted again, and I expected it'd found more kindling. Hopefully, it wasn't another ghoul.

"Is mage fire supposed to do that?" Caden whispered.

"No clue," I answered, to which, even in the dim light, I could make out his confused expression.

The fire engulfing the ghoul below sputtered. Would it explode soon too? The monster had reached Liam and lunged for the wolf, claws raised, and teeth bared. The snarl from its lips was otherworldly, full of an insatiable hunger.

Liam sidestepped the assault, and the ghoul, with its momentum, smashed into a boulder along the side of the trail, causing flares of mage fire to light up on impact. The fire faded in the ghoul's body afterward, as if the fire's substance had been squeezed out and left upon the rock, where it continued to blaze.

That was when I caught the glare of Marcos' eyes

reflecting the light from the mage fire moments before he landed on the beast. His impact drove the ghoul flat to the ground, his jaws clamped down on the back of the monster's neck like a vise. The remaining fire didn't deter him, and for a moment I wondered if he felt it at all.

The ghoul rallied, bucking Marcos off of him, but he was injured, his head torn part way off, now dangling at an angle. The monster lunged at Marcos, but Liam came up behind him, grabbing its hind foot in his jaws, holding the creature in place. Marcos rounded and swiped his paws at the ghoul, shredding through the last remaining tendons in its neck, and the head went flying. The body slumped to the ground; the undead monster now truly dead. Both the head and body continued to burn, the flames casting an eerie glow on the cliff side wall.

The moment passed. I breathed out a sigh of relief. To my surprise, tears ran down my cheeks, and I worked to wipe them away with my free hand.

"They did it," Franc whispered into my ear, giving my waist another squeeze before he let me go. "Didn't we say they could handle it?"

Liam and Marcos, both still in animal form, checked each other out, and then Marcos turned and jumped up onto the cliff ledge, much higher than I'd thought possible. Liam followed him up a moment later, jumping, bounding off of an outcropping of rock, and then completing the jump up.

It wasn't until they shifted back that I realized Marcos had burns up his right arm from fighting the ghoul. "Oh my gods, are you okay?"

"I'll heal quick enough," he replied, although he winced when he moved. Between the moonlight and the mage fire below, he was lucky the burns weren't more extensive. Marcos found his bag, pulled out his clothes, and got dressed.

"Can you do healing magic?" Caden asked me.

"No, that skill's not in my repertoire," I replied.

"Too bad Emrys isn't here," Franc replied. "He's got some limited skill in that arena. I think I saw a first aid kit in one bag." Franc went to retrieve it.

"We got off light," Liam said. He found his bag and then pulled on his clothes. "This cave is relatively defensible for tonight. If we wait to travel until daylight, we'll likely avoid more encounters with the undead."

"Can ghouls jump this high?" I asked Caden.

Caden shrugged. "No clue, but we have to assume it's possible. Let's hope no others show up, but we'll have to keep watch through the night to make sure."

"Here's some burn cream," Franc said, holding it out to Marcos, who took it and began applying a thin coating to his burns.

"I'll take the first watch," Marcos said. "It's not like I can sleep until this heals a bit."

"I'll sit with you," Liam said. "I've got too much adrenaline pumping anyway to sleep for a while."

"I don't imagine I can sleep either," I said, followed by a yawn. Taking a moment to check in with my body, I realized how exhausted I felt, even though my mind was still running in circles. A chill ran over my skin, and I remembered I was still in wet shoes and pants. "Besides, it's too cold."

"Doesn't help you're still in wet clothes and shoes. Here, I found some blankets and extra sets of clothes," Caden replied. "C'mon, let me show you."

Caden led me deeper into the cave to a flat area where he'd layered a couple of thin blankets to form a rudimentary sleeping pallet. I pulled off my shoes, socks, and pants.

"Here, try these on for size," Caden said. He handed me some leggings and fresh socks, which I tried out. I rarely slept in clothes, but as this cave didn't come with a heater, I'd adapt.

Caden took my wet clothes and hung them over rocky outcroppings on the cave wall to dry. It was a sweet gesture, something I hadn't quite expected from what I knew of him. Perhaps he was more than he seemed?

"Thanks, they seem to fit fine," I replied. "Taneisha really planned this out."

"It seems so," Caden replied.

Franc, who'd changed into fresh pants and nothing else, joined us. He crawled into the sleeping blankets, and then beckoned me over. "The night is wasting."

I hesitated for a moment. Did I really want to sleep next to these two? Neither Marcos nor Liam seemed to trust Caden, but it appeared Franc had no such qualms. The shifters had said these two were also my mates, so where did that leave me? Assuming I believed the markings on my skin, which I felt were dubious considering the timing of their appearance.

My body and mind were so exhausted, I brushed away my doubts for another day. I'd handle those questions tomorrow, assuming I didn't end up becoming a ghoul's dinner in the meantime. I laid down next to Franc, and he pulled me close, spooning against me like we'd done it a million times before.

"Is this comfortable for you?" he asked as he ran a

hand down my side, resting his hand on my leg.

I adjusted myself, positioning my arm under my head. "I wish I had a pillow."

"Try this." Franc pulled one bag over and used it for his own pillow, and then adjusted his arm under my head. Despite the ordeal we'd just endured, he smelled faintly of pine and bourbon.

"Thanks, that helps." I wrapped my arms around my torso, hoping to warm my chilled fingertips more quickly.

While we were getting situated, Caden changed into fresh pants and then joined us, sandwiching me between them. Franc pulled a blanket over us, cocooning me in relative warmth and safety. I shivered for a moment or two, but soon enough a languid warmth spread over me, and I relaxed against them both.

With Caden facing me, it was hard to know where to put my arms. I couldn't see his features that well in the darkness, but he smelled of sweat and musky incense. The combination of being surrounded by their scents and lying against their muscular bodies was downright erotic. I remembered how Franc had given Caden the blowjob back at the shed, and suddenly getting a few hours of sleep was the furthest thing from my mind.

We're supposed to be sleeping, I scolded myself.

I shifted, trying to feel more comfortable and settle myself down for sleep, despite sleep now being the last thing on my mind. Whichever way I adjusted, I couldn't help being wedged up between them. At first, I was just trying to get comfortable, but then I had to admit, some of my squirreling around was just reveling in the pure sensation of having them both right there.

I recalled, in a very visceral way, that Caden was an

incubus and Franc a demi-god hailing from Dionysos. They weren't trying to seduce me, yet here I was, getting myself worked up just from being near them. This pair was, literally, born to party. Too bad Taneisha's quest wasn't about who could party the hardest, because these two would have knocked that goal out of the park.

"Are you comfortable?" Caden whispered.

I felt the flush hit my cheeks. Lying here in the dark, I'd become lost in my own thoughts. Obviously, they'd noticed me squirming between them. "Not exactly. My arms are a little cramped."

"How about this?" He took hold of my wrist, guiding my arm over his torso and wrapping it around him. "You're welcome to cuddle up on me as much as you'd like." Caden's deep, raspy whisper evoked a shiver down my back.

Was it my temperature going up? Caden's? All of ours? At least I wasn't cold anymore.

"Could you roll onto your back?" I asked Caden.

He let out an affirmative rumble, rolled onto his back, and then slid back against me. I curled up across his chest, wrapped my arm around his torso, luxuriating in the feel of Caden's skin. Franc moved closer, spooning up against me in the most delicious way.

Franc ran the gentle pressure of his fingertips across my hip and thigh, awaking my skin and leaving a trail of tingles in his wake. Caden brought his hand up to my face and tucked my hair behind my ear, planting a sweet, and not at all demonish, kiss upon my forehead.

I relaxed against them, a heat building between my thighs. Despite my building desire, I lost consciousness as exhaustion overtook me.

BEWITCHED NIGHTS

CADEN

I awoke to someone writhing against me, and for a moment, I couldn't remember where I was or how I got here. My mental reflexes kicked in, primed for potential danger. The light was dim; the air smelled faintly of brimstone, and someone, or someone's, limbs splayed out over me.

If only I could say this was an unfamiliar experience.

But then, with a jolt, our present situation slammed into my mind. I remembered how the mage, Sera, had curled up against me. As an incubus demon, I was used to the arousal I elicited from others simply by existing. My charmed necklace muted, but didn't fully block my demonic abilities, meaning my powers wouldn't overwhelm those around me. Yet when people touched me, my powers became difficult to resist.

Which was why I'd expected Sera to initiate sex, but she didn't. Instead, she'd sought my comfort, of all things, in this hellish landscape. That guileless act softened my heart to her, despite her being a mage.

Then she'd fallen asleep, asking nothing more than my touch and the heat of my body against the night's chill. I'd followed her to dreamtime not long thereafter, eager to claim a few hours of needed rest, despite my desire to bury myself in her flesh. Now, all of my attention was focused on the way Sera pressed her thigh against my erection, grinding as she let out a breathy moan.

Under the thin blanket, I saw Franc run his hand up Sera's leg, resting it on the curve of her hip as he gently kneaded her flesh through the thin fabric of her leggings. I looked up and my gaze met his. From the familiar, heated look in his eyes, I knew I wasn't the only one sporting a hard on.

I brushed Sera's hair out of her face, revealing her full lips and long, dark lashes. I wanted nothing more than to ravish her with kisses from her nape to her toes.

I let out a heavy breath. Of course, I wanted Sera. How could I not? I loved to fuck. I lived to fuck. Sera was flirty as a kitten, confident as a lion, and fearless as a wolverine. Problem was, the mage was also clever as a fox, and so I had to keep her at arm's length, which meant no sex.

There was no way this mage was learning my secrets. And that mate mark? Clearly, Taneisha had somehow made that happen just to distract us from finding our legacies.

However, Franc wasn't privy to my internal monologue, and by the devilish glint in the demi-god of madness' eyes, I knew he was going to make things hard on me. Franc traced his fingers up Sera's back, and she shifted her weight even further onto me, letting out an almost purr-like groan as she nuzzled her face along my neck.

I turned to Sera just as she brought her face up, and our lips met as she claimed a hungry kiss. For a heartbeat of a moment, I froze, but then all thought fled. I gave into the sweetness of her taste, the near-electric feeling of her fingers razing against my chest, and the building, driving need for more.

And then a little more. Sera nipped at my bottom lip, and I grabbed her roughly, pressing her mouth against mine as I explored her with my tongue.

I knew I needed to stop, but I'd never been good at denying myself. What was one more grind of my hips? One more thrust of my tongue? One more taste of her skin?

I groaned in defeat. Using all of my mental fortitude, I disentangled myself from their embrace, rolled over, and sat up. Sera's disappointed sigh rang in my ears, beckoning me back. I reminded myself that I had to keep my distance from Sera. Besides, was she even into me, or just bewitched by my demonic powers?

"We should let the others get some sleep," I said to Franc.

"You're serious?" he asked. A combination of frustration and amusement filled his eyes. I watched as he withdrew his hand from Sera's stomach, gliding it along her hip as he watched my reaction.

Franc was such a tease, and normally I adored him for it. But I couldn't let him drive the action today.

"I am. Come on, Franc."

Sera nodded, as if I was making all the sense in the world and sat up. "Okay, okay. I'll get moving."

"No, Sera, get more sleep," I said. "It's still early."

Sera's pout and Franc's incredulous expression

followed me as I rose and walked toward the front of the cave, adjusting my aching cock along the way.

Marcos stood, leaning against the wall of the cave, looking out over the mountainside. Liam sat across the opening of the mouth of the cave facing Marcos, but with an eye to the valley below. He turned and watched me approach with a knowing gaze and a wry smile. I assumed he'd overheard everything, considering he had keen hearing, and the cave wasn't exactly that big.

"You get some rest?" Liam asked.

I walked up to the edge of the cliff, surveying the trail below. Although I'd grown up in New Orleans, my grandmother had brought me here to the Netherworld, the land of our people, on a handful of occasions. I wasn't sure last night, but now, I was certain. By the quality of the light, I knew we were in the pre-dawn hours. "Enough for the time being. You and Marcos should get a couple of hours in before we head out."

Liam stood up, stretching. "Don't mind if I do."

I tried not to imagine Sera wrapped around Liam and failed. Still, I'd pay good money for that show anytime. "You see anything?"

"We heard ghouls in the distance. A couple approached the mage fire at the river, but then wandered off. One we saw nosing around at the ghoul corpse remnants on the road. None of them ventured further up this way," Marcos replied.

Franc lumbered out from the back, walking stiffly from the rough sleeping. He cracked his neck, letting out a sigh of relief.

"That good?" Marcos asked him.

Franc flashed us his demure 'don't you wish you were me,' smile. "Cave sleeping has its charm."

I think we all knew he meant Sera's company. At least, I got the joke, but I wasn't laughing.

Marcos knocked knuckles with Franc and then headed towards the back of the cave. Towards Sera. I rarely felt jealous. Demons weren't wired for it, particularly incubi. The more in the party, the more I fed off the raw lust. Yet now I experienced a momentary pang of... well, something.

"We found some snack bars and canteens in the packs," Liam said. "Nothing much to get excited about, but at least we don't have to hunt down food."

"Lucky. This realm is low on grocery stores."

"Bars too?" Franc asked.

I chucked. "Depends on what you like to drink?"

Liam gave us a nod and then headed to join Sera and Marcos. I leaned against the cave opening, determined not to think about what I might miss out on.

Franc sauntered over and stood close to me. "What's up with your mood today?"

"Nothing's up with me."

He rolled his eyes. "I can tell when you're moping about something because your dimple shows. Plus, you passed up on a prime opportunity to feed back there. What gives?"

"I don't have a dimple. You must be thinking of someone else."

Franc reached up, brushed his thumb across my dimpled cheek, and then cupped the back of my neck with his hand. I hoped he'd move in, crushing me beneath a passionate kiss with his need, but he maintained the space between us. We were on watch duty, after all. I needed to keep my head in the game. The saving Emrys from the fae dungeon game.

"I know everything about you, demon." A glitter of intimate knowledge lit up Franc's eyes, and for a moment my thoughts turned downright carnal. "So why didn't you let that hot little witch mount you like the stallion you are?"

I raised my brows. "Sera wasn't even fully awake. I bet she thought I was someone else. Someone shiftery."

He tilted his head to the side, a smile playing over his lips. "Are you not interested in the mage?"

I shrugged. "What if I'm not?"

Franc dropped his hand from my neck and crossed his arms. "I thought incubi were pansexual. Omni sexual? Everything sexual?"

"Oh, come on, it's not like I'll bang just anything. I have taste."

"I've witnessed a few of your refined sensibilities at my club." His gaze narrowed on me. "But it's Sera you don't find worthy of your infernal affections?"

Ouch! Not that I could argue his point. I'd partied with some pretty questionable characters and Franc's club had been the spot I often used to meet them.

I held up my hands. "That's not what I meant. Of course, she's worthy. It's just…"

"I cannot wait to hear what makes a charmer like Sera so unfuckable. I mean, she was amazing to watch. Have you imagined what it would be like for us to have her together? Or all of us together?"

I blew out a heavy sigh. Leave it to the party god to pave the way into this conversation. Sure, we'd partied plenty with the posse back in the day, but never sharing just one woman between us. I doubted the shifters would go for that. Liam had practically already sunk his teeth into her already.

"It's those mating marks, okay. I have abso-fucking-lutely zero interest in being mated off by fate, no thank you very much."

"Oh." Franc scoffed. "You really think those are real and not just some fae trickery?"

"I'm not willing to take a chance. Fated mates is a hard limit for me."

"That's uncharacteristically cautious of you," Franc said. "I can't imagine how fated mates would work for me, either. My life doesn't exactly scream committed relationship material."

"These are strange times," I replied. "Now, if it were fated fucks, I'd be down in a heartbeat."

"There's my demon," Franc grinned at me.

"We should focus on watching the trail," I said, hoping to shut down the conversation. I couldn't dance around my denied attraction to Sera forever. Franc knew me well enough that he'd eventually figure out I was keeping something.

"Whatever you want. But I will say, I'm surprised you're showing so much restraint."

"I have to. Emrys' life is on the line, as are my grandmother's sacred huppulu seeds." Seeds I'd stolen to show off to the posse. "I'm sufficiently motivated."

"None of us will risk Emrys, Caden," Franc replied. "You'd be stronger after sex though, am I right?"

Was he offering? Wait, no. It didn't matter. We were on guard duty, for hell's sake.

"Keep your eyes on the road, party god."

Franc shook his head and backed up, hands in the air. "Okay, okay. I'll let up. For now."

"That's better than I'd expected."

DEMON DAYS

CADEN

We sat in silence for a few hours, watching the sun rise over the landscape below. I pulled the map I'd found yesterday out and studied it, becoming more and more convinced I knew just where we were. By the time Marcos, Liam, and a sleepy-eyed Sera emerged from the darkness of the depths of the cave, it had to be close to ten.

I couldn't know for certain, but I could almost always scent the potency of recent sex on someone. Sexual essence was an intoxicant to my kind, urging us to feed on the sexual energy. But by the mood hanging on those three, they hadn't indulged. A pity, that. At least someone should have. Then I could have gotten buzzed by the mere aura of their sensual energy.

"See anything?" Liam asked.

"Just the daylight burning away," Franc replied. He stood calmly, staring off into the distance. "We should get moving soon."

Sera, still in her t-shirt, leggings, and socks, planted her hands on her hips. "Not so fast, Franc. First, we need a plan."

"The plan, little mage, is to climb the mountain and recover Caden's seeds, or were you not paying attention?" Franc asked.

She marched right up to Franc, raised her chin, and looked him right in the eye. He was a good foot taller than her, but she didn't appear intimidated by his Viking-esque frame. All signs of her prior exhaustion had faded.

"That's not a plan."

Franc's gaze swept over Sera, amusement playing over his features. "Do you have a better game plan?"

Marcos, who had been rummaging through the bags, approached Sera, and handed her some clothes. "Pants?"

"Yes, pants first. Thanks, Marcos." Sera swiped them from him but kept her focus on Franc. "I have a plan besides pants. Can we all sit and plan for just like five minutes?" she asked, stepping into black pants as Marcos steadied her with his hand.

"No," I said. "Franc's right. Daylight is burning, and five minutes could easily become an hour." Sera planted her hands on her hips, and I knew I needed to give her a better reason. "Look, I've been studying the map, and we need to get a move on, especially if we hope to get lucky with another safer spot to camp when night falls."

Sera glanced around the cave and then relented. "Fine. We can walk and talk and plan. Now that we have daylight, what goodies is everyone finding in the backpacks Taneisha gave us?"

Each of us dug into our bags, doing a quick inventory.

"I've got a water bottle, a folding knife, some protein bars, a spare set of clothing, a jacket, and a lightweight blanket," Liam said. "There are some general toiletries, including sunscreen and bug spray. And a white bandana?"

"Same," Marcos said. "At least we won't starve or freeze to death."

I nodded, as did Franc and Sera.

"There's a box of matches and a flashlight too in my gear," Liam added.

"That's just you. I have binoculars," Franc added. "And gum?"

"I don't have those, but I've got a hatchet, some rope, and a first aid kit," Marcos said.

"I've got a multi-tool, hand sanitizer, and a tarp," I added. "Am I the only one who got condoms?"

"No, but you're the only one to mention them. I also have duct tape," Sera said, barking out a laugh. "Everything's better with duct tape."

"Everything?" I asked. The word slipped out before I could stop myself. Hell, Caden! I thought I wasn't flirting with the little mage.

Sera's mouth formed a little "o" as she digested my question. "Uh, no. Definitely not everything."

Liam grabbed some snack bars and passed them around as we picked out our clothes for the day, finished dressing, and re-packed our bags.

Franc got out his binoculars and surveyed the horizon. "Nothing's moving and the mage fire is still burning."

Sera nodded, but when she spoke, she didn't address his comment. "Then let's get going."

We tossed our bags down over the short cliff to the trail below, and then Franc and I lowered ourselves down, making the fall manageable. Liam lowered Sera down to

Franc and my waiting arms, preventing her from taking a tumble. The shifters lowered themselves, landing much more gracefully than the demi-god and I had managed.

We shouldered our backpacks and continued up the mountain trail, falling into an easy rhythm with Liam and Marcos taking the lead. The cold, grey color of the rocky hillside was dotted with a smattering of scrub brush and boulders. Despite the desolation of this place, there was this well-worn trail. I knew from the map that it led up and over a ridge before entering a valley containing a river, followed by another steep incline up the mountain.

Sera had tied a bandana around her wrist, perhaps to keep it close at hand? I looked around and noticed Franc had tied his loosely around his neck, while Marcos wore his as a headband. Liam had his at the ready, stuffed mostly into his jeans pocket. Who knew bandanas were so popular? I'd left mine in my backpack.

Sera came to walk alongside me and turned to me. The sheer ferocity of her brown-eyed gaze astonished me. I should have expected it from her. It's not like she was just some human woman in Franc's club looking for a good time. Seraphina was a mage of the Lowe family, renowned for their power. In this moment, despite sleeping rough and no doubt still sleep deprived, she held herself with the grace of someone used to wielding authority.

Her self-assuredness was such a turn on.

"What can you tell us about this place?"

Despite the intensity of her gaze, a nagging thought tugged at my thoughts. Why had Sera's mage fire been so wild last night? If I took her offhand comment as honesty, she hadn't entirely known how the mage fire would behave. How could a mage not know how their magic would perform? Was that typical mage guile, sarcasm, or was there more going on here?

"Caden?" she asked, bringing my thoughts back to her question. "Do you know where we are and who we're up against?"

"We're in the Netherworld. I think," I explained. "I can't know for sure, but with the ghouls and the quality of the light, all read as the demon dimension to me. I recognize a few landmarks on the map. Plus, it just... smells like I remember."

"Then you've been here before?"

"If it's indeed the Netherworld, then yeah. Granny Lily brings me here every few years. It's a forced pilgrimage to reconnect with my roots or some such bullshit."

"Granny? Okay, let's go with that," Sera said. "Taneisha said someone stole your legacy from her and that they live at the top of a tall mountain. She dropped us here, so it's safe to assume this is this place. Since it's your legacy, I assume you'll have a clue where we are. What do you know about this mountain and this mystery thief?"

I ran a hand through my hair, but the black strands fell right back into my eyes. "The landscape here is pretty bleak. Not much grows or lives in the demon realm, and what does... Well, you've seen a sampling. Anything that can make it here has a bite."

"Some of us more than others," Liam replied. He was walking in front of us but turned back and flashed a smug smile that said, 'bring it on.' And why not? He and Marcos had proven their abilities in the fight last night against the ghoul.

"Anyway," I continued. I chose not to take Marcos' remark personally. I knew I wasn't much of a fighter, although I could hold my own in a scrap when I had to. I was a lover, sustaining myself by feeding on lust and desire. But those, too, could be weaponized. "There's an ancient myth about this mountain, specifically the tallest mountain in the Netherworld. They say a creature named the Anzu lives in dominion here above all others, answering to no one. It's half bird, half man, and all demon."

"How strong is it? Like, an immortal, or does it just have a super high constitution?" Sera asked.

"High constitution?" Was that a mage term? "Pardon?"

Sera shook her head. "Never mind. What else can you tell us about the Anzu?"

I racked my brain for details about the ancient creature. "The monster has power over the wind and thunder. It likes to steal things and hide them on its mountaintop."

"How hard is it to kill?" she asked.

"I don't think we can. I mean, it's killed in multiple myths. Sometimes by gods. Sometimes arrows. So, it's possible, but it always comes back."

"So, it's more like a phoenix?" Franc asked.

"Maybe? Look, history lessons were never my strong suit."

"What was?" Marcos said under his breath, just loud enough for everyone to hear.

The panther and I had never been close, but in the years since attending Goldenbriar academy together, we'd drifted even further apart. He wasn't wrong. I'd never been a strong student. Considering that he worked security for Franc's club, where I regularly brought trouble through the door, there was bound to be friction between us.

"That attitude doesn't help," Sera said, shutting Marcos down. I could hear the exhaustion in her voice. "We're here to retrieve Caden's legacy and save Emrys. Can we all agree to set aside differences and focus on that goal for now?"

We hit a switchback and turned with the path. The turn was steeper than the straightaways, so we all quieted with the added exertion until we'd rounded the bend.

"I'm sorry, Sera, I can't just let my concerns around Caden go," Marcos replied. "You haven't been around our posse for a while, but things aren't as simple as they were back at the academy. We're not the same tight-knit group from back then."

"I wouldn't expect that from any party, especially not with a group of supes," she replied, shaking her head. "Let's get our cards on the table. What's your beef with Caden?"

Marcos turned and looked me in the eye, but then kept on walking. "When we were younger, I never thought much about Caden being an incubus. He was the life of the party, and that's all that mattered to me then. But over the past few years while I've worked security for Velvet, I can't ignore the characters he surrounds himself with. I've thrown out his 'friends' time and time again for peddling illegal supe drugs, starting fights, and harassing other customers, especially the ladies. We've had the supe authorities out at least every other week arresting his 'friends.' Honestly, I don't understand why you keep letting him return, Franc."

Thing was, Marcos wasn't wrong. I'd brought plenty of delinquents and dealers into Velvet. But his distrust didn't hurt my feelings one bit. They didn't know my reasoning. All that mattered to me was having Franc's trust.

"That's between Caden and I," Franc replied. "He has leave to conduct his business as he wishes within Velvet."

Franc had never asked me why I kept the company I did, despite the regular disruptions to his business. Did he just tolerate my indiscretions? Or did Franc guess at my true goals? Either way, his trust meant the world to me.

Marcos scoffed. "Yeah, I know. It's your club, your rules, but I don't have to like it."

"That's right, you don't," Franc replied, his tone cool as a cucumber.

We trudged through a few moments of silence as we huffed around the next switchback.

"So, Marcos, what are you worried about now? Today? With this quest?" Sera asked, every few words punctuated by gulps of air.

I appreciated the mage's focus on the present moment. There was no way to heal the damage between Marcos and me, not unless I came clean with him about why my associates were so often of the criminal variety. I wasn't about to do that, not unless I had to.

Marcos stopped short, bringing their line to a halt, and faced me. I kept walking, coming face to face with him, so he could vent right to my face. "I'm worried you're going to give in to your demonic ways and one or more of us will get hurt. I'm worried we might screw up again and Emrys will pay the price. Mostly, I don't feel like I can trust you to act with the welfare of the rest of us in mind."

Fair enough. "I swear to you, Marcos, I won't bring any harm to any of us, not the posse nor Sera, by action or inaction," I said. "My goal is to help overcome Taneisha's quests, and I will forego my personal safety if I have to in order to make that happen."

Marcos frowned, his lips creasing into a tight line, as he looked me over. I knew he wouldn't believe me, but at least we'd aired our differences and maybe that would help lower tensions between us.

"Do any of you truth-speak?" Sera asked. We all shook our heads. "Then Caden's vow is all we can ask, and it's good enough for me. Marcos?"

"I guess it'll have to be good enough," Marcos muttered.

"Good. Let's keep going," Liam said, pulling Marcos by the sleeve. The panther shifter relented, and I let out the breath I didn't realize I'd been holding.

We kept our pace up the trail as we neared the last of the switchbacks. "The trail flattens out up ahead when we reach the river."

"Let me guess," Franc replied. "We get to cross it?"

I nodded. "Yes, assuming we want to keep going up."

"Can't say I do, but it's the task ahead of us," Sera said. She turned to me. "Tell me about this legacy of yours that's so cool that a mythical bird man steals it from faery and flies it to the top of a mountain."

I sighed. What to share? What to hold back? When I'd waffled long enough, Liam spoke up.

"Caden's family legacy is a small vase full of seeds which he temporarily liberated from his granny," Liam said. "I gave him crap about just showing off some seeds, but it appears those little grains were actually worth something."

"That's gracious of you, wolf," I snapped back. Liam

gave me a little bow with a flourish. "Jackass," I whispered, knowing he would hear me.

"What seeds?" Sera asked me, ignoring our banter.

"They're from the huppulu tree, which is sacred to my kind," I explained. "They are a symbol of a time when demons held power, not just in the Netherworld, but in the human world as well."

"It's like the strength and pride of your ancestors," Sera said. "I bet granny'll be pissed you lost them?"

I gritted my teeth. Sera had no idea. "You haven't lived until you've seen Granny Lily on a demon-fueled tirade."

She let out a weak laugh. "I'll pass on that, thanks. Why do you think the Anzu stole the seeds?"

I shrugged. "Since their origin is the underworld, they radiate an infernal energy. It's possible that's how the Anzu found them, even within faery."

As I finished speaking, Liam and Marcos reached the plateau where the trail leveled out.

"What in the hellfire is that?" Marcos spat out, standing stock-still with a silent Liam at his side.

We were a few paces behind the shifters, and when we topped the rise, the river came fully into view in the slight valley below. The rushing, roiling water bisected the valley, the trail continuing up the mountain on the far side.

The river was just where I'd expected it to be according to the map, except there was nothing ordinary about that water. I'd seen the river of creation before, yet I still wasn't prepared for its appearance. The silvery waters looked like a mix of liquid mercury with moving forms bubbling up under the surface, shifting and sliding over each other. When I focused on the movement, I could make out shapes. Shapes of something, or someone's, underneath the currents.

"Yeah, what he said," Franc added, hitching his thumb at Marcos. "What the fuck is that, Caden?"

I chose my next words carefully. Whatever happened, I had to convince everyone to cross together.

RIVER OF THE DEAD

SERA

I couldn't tear my gaze away from the roiling, quicksilver surface of the river.

"It's the river of creation," Caden answered in a 'duh' tone.

Liam's face screwed up with indignation. "Seriously? Like, how could we be expected to know that?"

The demon shrugged. "You studied harder than I did. Anyway, I think that's what granny called it. I've only been here once before. Also, I'd recommend not looking directly at it."

"Why? Is the water dangerous to stare at?" Liam asked.

"Nah, just creepy as hell." Caden answered, drawing a chuckle out of Franc and a grim nod from Liam.

"Is the water alive?" I asked.

"No? Sort of?" he replied. When everyone turned to look at Caden, his shoulders slumped and then he blew out a heavy breath. "Maybe? It's filled with demon wraiths, but that's not important right now."

"Not important?" I planted my hands on my hips. "If

we're going to wade through that crap, I'd say the demon water bears a smidge more explanation."

"Ew, no! We won't get into it," Caden replied, his features scrunching up in distaste. "We'll take the ferry."

He motioned to the river, and when I glanced back, there was a man, or creature, wrapped in tattered black robes that moved according to an unseen wind. His face was hidden in shadow, but he emanated malevolence. The figure stood, unmoving, atop a stone in the river. Had that rock been there a moment ago? The creature certainly hadn't been. The hair on my hairs stood on end and a chill crept across my skin, leaving a trail of goosebumps in its wake.

"You'd said we were in the Netherworld, but somehow seeing the ferryman makes things more real," I admitted.

Franc placed a comforting hand on my shoulder. The proximity to the demi-god triggered images of me, half asleep, nestled between Caden and Franc. What I wouldn't give to be sleeping comfortably in a bed between, well, any of my Supernova of Hotness guys rather than trekking through the wilderness of the Netherworld.

Was it too much to ask Taneisha to give us a quest based in a coffee shop, followed by a spa, an ice cream parlor, a bookstore, and then ending in a wine bar? Perhaps the quest for the perfect cinnamon roll?

Damn, I missed home.

"Tell me about it." Franc nodded. "So what's the game to ride the ride? Does Mr. Tall, Dark, and Ominous charge a fare?"

"Sort of," Caden replied, turning and walking towards the river.

I was glad I still had my purse, which I'd stowed in my

backpack. "I've got a handful of coins jangling around the bottom of my purse," I offered. "I could dig them out?"

Caden's expression knit with confusion, but then he smiled, his icy blue eyes glinting with amusement. "Don't bother. The ferryman doesn't take earthly money. He prefers blood offerings."

I shivered with revulsion. What did I expect in hell?

"You sure about that?" Marcos pressed.

Caden shrugged. "Yeah, as far as I remember."

Marcos frowned, clearly not happy with Caden's answer. "Then aren't we lucky all of our hearts are pumping? Let's just hope your memory is on point." Marcos turned and marched his way over to the ferryman. "Let's get this over with."

Marcos' grumpy attitude grated on me. I knew he didn't trust Caden, and he certainly had his reasons, but what choice did we have with Taneisha pulling our strings? Surely, the demon was more motivated to make it through this quest than any of us?

I followed the others, my skin crawling whenever I looked at the water or the ghostly ferryman. I had to keep Marcos in the game, despite his frustration with Caden.

The ferryman didn't move as we approached. His long, ephemeral robes floated as if ungoverned by gravity. Even as we approached, his face remained hidden within the deep cowl of his robe.

The water, however, gained an uncomfortable level of definition. While from a distance I'd been able to make out human-like forms undulating under the surface, now at the water's edge, I could count fingers. Teeth. Eyes. Horns. All flowing in and out of definition as the liquid rushed past us.

Caden walked right up to the ferryman. "How does this work again?"

The ferryman held out his hand, but didn't speak.

"Right. Here goes nothing."

Caden pulled out his folding knife, flicked it open, and then in a flash of steel drew the blade across his palm. As he raised his bleeding hand over the ferryman's, a stream of crimson blood fell. I'd expected some would hit the stone he was standing upon or the water, but the demon's blood defied gravity, flowing towards the cloaked figure's open palm. When the blood reached the ferryman's open hand, it absorbed, leaving no trace.

"Here I thought things couldn't get any creepier," Franc said softly. I felt like nodding, but I couldn't take my eyes off of the blood transaction happening right before my eyes.

The ferryman gestured with his free hand. His platform of stone expanded, just a little, and he crooked his finger.

"You first, Franc," Caden said, his hand continuing to trickle.

Franc frowned, but then nodded. He stepped over the space between the riverbank and the ferryman's platform. Was it just my overblown imagination, or had tendrils of silvered water reached up towards him as he passed over? Surely not. Yet a shiver ran down my spine and my nervous energy caused a spark of purple magic to dance around my fingertips. I balled up my fists, hoping no one would notice.

The ferryman gestured again, and again the rock platform expanded.

"You next, Liam," Caden said.

Liam's expression was no less grim, but he joined Franc on the platform a moment later.

Caden continued to bleed. How deep had he cut, and how long would it take to heal?

"Why only your blood?" I asked. "Why not each of us individually?"

"I'm buying us passage to the demonic Netherworld," Caden replied. "You're all coming along on the journey my blood dictates. It's the only way to go together to where the Anzu lives. Otherwise, the ferryman would take you to whichever afterlife your blood calls for."

"I thought we were already in the Netherworld?" I muttered.

Caden wobbled his head from side to side. "I call it all the Netherworld, but we've been crossing the mudroom to the proper entrance, more or less. It's your turn now, Sera."

Damn. I nibbled my lip as I stepped over the writhing river. There was no mistaking how tiny tentacles reached up for me. I rushed the second step, bumping into Liam, who caught me with a firm grip.

"I won't let you fall," he whispered, his breath hot against my ear.

I looked up into his emerald green eyes. His heart was right there at the surface, begging for me to claim him as my own. "I know."

Liam was easy to trust. I never had to wonder where he stood. He was utterly transparent about what he felt and thought. It didn't hurt that the rest of the posse appeared to trust him implicitly. It felt almost too easy with the wolf shifter. I felt like I could fall for him way too fast.

I stayed next to Liam, but turned back to watch Marcos step onto the stone pier after me. Caden continued to bleed into the ferryman's hand, waiting his turn. His behavior continued to not fit the impression Marcos had painted of him. Right now, Caden was literally sacrificing his life's blood for all of us on this mission. Sure, the goal was to save his sacred demon seeds, but we were also working to save Emrys.

The last cost of admission felt like it took longer. Was Caden bleeding slower, or the ferryman holding out? I had no way of knowing. My fingers dug into the arm Liam had wound around my middle, and he gave me a comforting squeeze. When Caden eventually stepped onto the rock safely beside us, I let out a long sigh.

Despite our dire circumstances, there was a glimmer of amusement in Caden's eyes. "Worried for me, little mage?"

"I'd hate to get stuck in the Netherworld without you, if that's what you mean."

I thought I glimpsed a sad frown play across his features. There one moment and gone the next. Had I imagined it? Had I upset the bravado-filled demon's feelings?

"Then you're in luck," he answered, but his usual witty snap wasn't there.

The ferryman turned to face the other shore, basically ignoring us now that Caden had paid for our passage. A moment later, the earth shook under us as the entire platform of rock jolted into action.

"The rock is the raft?" Marcos blurted out, his voice higher pitched than I'd heard it before.

"Don't worry, pussycat," Caden replied. "You'll make it across dry."

Marcos shot Caden a withering stare, silencing the demon. Seriously, maybe they needed to go at it and work their shit out? There was only so long you could hold that strained posturing before something broke.

"Take a deep breath," Liam said, his breath warm against my ear.

Like I was the one who needed to chill out?

"Why?" I asked. "I'm doing fine." Or so I thought.

Liam glanced down at my hands, which sparkled with power. I balled my hands into fists, tucking them against my body, but the light purple flares didn't let up.

"You're safe," Liam said, his voice gentle. "At least, as safe as you can be on the ferryman's raft in hell."

I flashed him a forced smile. "I know that. At least, I think I do." So why couldn't I keep my eyes from straying to the undead demon infested water roiling around us? "Look at it," I pointed to the water. "It might be my overactive imagination, but I think that demon-water is curling up onto our ferry."

Caden's attention was already on the river, but Franc and Marcos both looked at where I was pointing.

"I think it just does that," Caden said. "It seems rhythmic. Like little waves."

Marcos flashed him a glare. "Almost sounds like you like it."

The look Caden gave Marcos was devoid of emotion, but his body posture was tense. "There's beauty in life and death."

"How much longer before we're across?" I asked, hoping to shift the conversation.

The guys all looked over at the far bank, but it was Caden who answered. "Another minute. We've already passed the midway point."

"Not much of a river," I said. "If it weren't for the demons, we could swim across."

"And if it weren't for faeries, we wouldn't be here at all," Franc mumbled.

Liam gripped me tight around my waist. "I, for one, am glad we're here," he murmured into my ear, sending a thrill down my spine.

"Cool it with the mating talk, wolf. It's the last thing we need to be thinking about right now," Franc said, his tone brooking no argument.

"We're not in your club, Franc. You're not in charge here," Liam replied.

Franc pushed past Marcos, coming face to face with Liam. Franc's face was flushed. "Neither are you. We should focus on saving Emrys, not who's banging her mageness here."

"Hey," I yelled. "I'm right here, you know."

"No offense, Sera," Franc said, but his focus remained on Liam.

I couldn't see Liam's expression, but his body was taut and primed to hold his ground. I tried to pull away, but Liam wasn't about to loosen his grip on me.

Right at that moment, a few things went wrong all at once. Something brushed the fingertips of my right hand, and I swear my heart skipped a beat. I jerked away, glancing down to see tiny tentacles reaching up towards me from the murky waters, as if drawn to the glow of the uncontrolled magic bleeding from my fingertips. Off balance, I jerked away from Liam, but he struggled to keep his grip on me, unaware of the cause of my alarm.

When I broke free, I smashed into Franc. The extra oomph from the magic coursing through my body threw him back just a few feet. Problem was, because of the close quarters, he stumbled backwards into Marcos, pushing him back as well. Marcos slipped backwards further than we had ferry, slipping off the edge and into the foul river. A flash of raw panic flooded his features as his fingers clawed against the smoothed rock surface of our ferry.

"Marcos!" I yelled, heart in my chest.

Franc and Caden both lunged for him. They each got one of Marcos' arms and pulled, dragging him partially back onto the safety of the stone, although his lower half still hung in the river. The silvered water of the river clung to Marcos' body, wrapping its blackened tentacles around him, unwilling to release its prize. We were now only fifteen feet from the shore, but it might as well be a mile if we couldn't free Marcos from the undead demons.

"Keep pulling!" I cried.

Franc and Caden seemed to understand the undead waters had no intention of giving up, and continued pulling Marcos up onto the ferry. The undead tentacles gave no appearance of relinquishing their prey. For every inch they pulled Marcos out, they lost half that distance as the river fought back.

I raised my hands, which glowed with an electric charge fueled by my fear alone. Would my magic bend to my will in our time of need? Knowing Marcos was in the water because of me, his very life in the balance, I couldn't just stand by and do nothing.

"Mojo, don't fail me now," I whispered. I let loose a series of lightning bursts aimed straight at the water near Marcos' feet. On impact, my magic lit up white-hot veins across the surface of the water, covering the roiling black waves between us and the shore. An ethereal screech pierced the air, coming from nowhere and everywhere.

Marcos yelped in pain, but then a moment later the demonic tentacles retreated all at once, freeing his legs. Franc and Caden fell back on their butts as they gave one last heave, pulling Marcos fully up onto the safety of the ferry. The surface of the water shuddered and twitched, the fan-like pattern of my electric magic burning its way across the surface.

The three men, brothers of choice, checked each other out. Franc pulled Marcos close, holding him tight for a brief but heartfelt moment. I'd witnessed plenty of their joking camaraderie, witty banter, and even heated arguments. This was the first opportunity I'd had to see them be gentle with each other, and it was a relief to see, especially between Caden and Marcos.

I felt a spark of hope. Perhaps there was room for them to move past their distrust of each other, after all?

Relieved to see Marcos safe and exhausted by my brief but intense effort, I stumbled backward, right into Liam's steady arms.

"I've got you," he said, holding me tight. I slumped against his strength, more tired than I thought I had a right to be.

I looked at my hands, silently thanking my magic for behaving at such a critical moment.

"We're almost to the other side," Caden said. He rose to his feet, rubbing his shoulder, before offering Marcos a hand up. "Let's clear out of here as quickly as we can."

Marcos, his lips a thin line as his jaw twitched, accepted Caden's help, but he was unsteady on his feet, favoring his left leg. His black jeans and boots looked intact, but I worried what injuries he might have sustained in the encounter. Franc moved in close, stabilizing him.

"I'm sorry I knocked you off. The tentacles were grabbing at my hand and I freaked out," I said to Marcos, feeling my heart in my throat. Franc flashed me a withering look, but held his tongue. "Are you hurt?"

"I'll be okay, Sera," Marcos said.

When he stretched out his leg, wincing from the movement, I wasn't so sure.

Franc took a couple of steps closer to me, again getting up in my face. "I'm over your mysterious and unstable magic." I could see the pain in Franc's face and his distrust was palpable. "You're going to need to come clean with us, mage. I want to know why the river was so attracted to you."

The pain in his eyes kicked me in the gut. Marcos and Liam knew about my magic, but my unwillingness to explain to the others had endangered them. I nodded. "I will. I swear it."

The ferry came to a stop with a jolt as it hit the shore. Relief washed over me as we disembarked, the ferryman paying us little to no mind. Every step away from the river lowered my anxiety. When we stopped to look back, the ferry and the ferryman had disappeared.

The effect of my magic remained visible on the surface of the water, which was now uncannily still. A network of lightning electric fire pulsed across the surface, the magical energy continuing to spend itself. Then as I watched, the network of capillaries flashed a bright purple light, and split open, oozing out upon the surface.

"It's as if the color black rotted and oozed, and then got even blacker," Liam said.

"That can't be good," Marcos said, voicing what we were all thinking.

The threads of blacker than black ooze moved across the quicksilver surface of the water, shuddering like worms caught in puddles after a sudden rain.

"Which is why we need a full explanation of your magic," Franc said to me. "For now, let's get away from whatever fresh hell is unearthing there."

Eager to put some distance between us and the undead demon water, we headed up the steep, but deserted, trail up the mountain. The trail was more narrow than before, so Liam and I took the lead. Franc walked next to Marcos, who refused his aid, while Caden took up the rear.

"I can't help but wonder if Taneisha lied to us," Liam said to me.

"What do you mean?" I asked. "Do you think Caden's seeds aren't here?"

"No, I think perhaps she allowed them to be taken by, or gave them to, the Anzu. I doubt the beast stole them from her." Liam scraped a hand across his face, wiping away beads of sweat.

I held my hand to my chest, mocking shock. "You'd accuse a fae of lying?"

Liam rewarded me with a wisp of a smile. "Of course I would. I refuse to believe we've ended up here by chance."

"This place is so dangerous, though," I said. "Sending us here on purpose would mean Taneisha wanted to risk us."

By the wary look in his eyes, I'd understood Liam's meaning. "That's exactly my thinking. We need to be very careful or the fae's game could quickly turn deadly."

NOT ALL WHO WANDER ARE LOST

FRANC

"What can we expect around the next turn?" I asked Caden, who was poring over the singular map the faery had deigned to bestow upon us.

Somehow, the incubus could hike up the trail while reading the map, even despite our grueling pace. I was impressed, but also worried about his safety. I had to imagine that this descent into hell was harder on Caden than the rest of us, not just because his legacy was on the line, but also because of his family history here.

Hell, I worried about everyone's welfare, even the little secretive mage with the luscious curves.

My gaze drifted to Sera for a moment, drinking in the cadence of her steps and the sway of her hips. Boy, did I love those curves. But that didn't mean I was going to let Sera get away with hiding something from the posse. My brothers of choice came first. Always.

Caden swept his black hair back and out of his face, roughly tucking it behind his ear. It was such a simple gesture. One I'd seen him do hundreds, if not thousands, of times. He looked wound up and in dire need of release. A bad idea for anyone, but even worse for our incubus. The last thing we needed was an explosion of his sexual energy at an inopportune moment.

At least I knew how to help Caden pass that hurdle.

"After the delightful slog up this rocky, poorly maintained path, we cross through another pass and a traverse before heading," he glanced up at me, a glint of humor in his eyes. "You guessed it. Up again."

"Delightful is not the word I'd use for it," I muttered. "I'm more interested in the landmarks called out on the map. Is there any detail on the traverse?"

He referenced the map again, beads of sweat visible on his brow. "It's named 'The Narrows', so I imagine it's even less wide than this section. Don't worry, we'll find out soon enough. We're almost there."

"Are there any way stations noted on the maps? It would be good to plan for safe spots to rest."

Caden shook his head as he folded up the map, tucking it back into a side pocket in his backpack. "Resting is the last thing we need to be doing out in the open in the Netherworld. The longer we're here, the more trouble will find us. We're better off pushing through so we can get out of here."

"Won't do us any good if we get hurt," I countered.

"Injuries heal." Caden grimaced, looking like he'd bitten into something bitter. "I'd rather deal with someone getting hurt if it means Taneisha returns Emrys to us safely."

I held his gaze for a moment, just long enough to

realize just how serious he was. "Fair enough. No dawdling. Check."

I looked around, searching for something that might speak to my wild, forest-fueled soul, some lifeblood of nature I could tap into, but I found little to celebrate. This part of the mountain was devoid of trees and almost all signs of life, unless you counted the ghouls or the undead demons in the river. The only regular foliage consisted of spindly squat briars dotting the hillside on both sides of the trail, as barren as the surrounding land. The lack of trees meant we had an expansive view of the desolate valley below, but that wasn't something I'd count as much of a blessing.

I focused on my footing and keeping a steady pace, and before long, we'd reached an area where the trail leveled out again. Everyone seemed to see it as an opportunity to take a breather before ploughing through the next section of trail.

After gulping down water from her water bottle, Sera wandered a little further ahead. Was she keeping her distance from me after I'd called her out on holding out on us with her magical problems?

Let her try. I wouldn't let this go, so she'd be singing like a siren eventually. I smiled to myself, imagining the possibilities. Perhaps in more ways than one.

Stretching my arms and taking a pull of water, I turned away and looked back the way we'd come, appreciating the height and distance travelled, which I felt in my bones and sore muscles. That was when I noticed something out of the corner of my eye. An inky black movement on the trail below, there one second and gone the next.

I blinked my eyes and wiped the sweat off my brow. Perhaps I'd imagined it?

No, there it was again. "Guys?" I called out, searching the trail for another glimpse. "Well, guys and lady. We've got a problem."

Caden was at my side a moment later, looking at where I was pointing. "What now?"

I shook my head. "I'm not sure, but I saw movement on the trail below."

Liam joined us, and we were silent for a moment as we scanned the landscape for movement.

"You could just say, 'hey posse,' you know?" Sera said.

I cast my gaze back over my shoulder at her. Marcos was sitting on a short boulder, looking like he was still in pain, and Sera stood next to him. Was I imagining it, or was she hovering over him? A flash of discomfort snaked through me. She was quickly becoming entangled with our posse and I wasn't sure how comfortable I was with this new turn of events.

Our posse had grown so far apart these past few years. I'd counted myself lucky when everyone, even Liam, could make it to the party I'd set up in their honor. It felt truly like old times, at least it had before Taneisha had stolen our legacies. I hadn't even worried about the prospect of group quests.

But that was before the fae had sent us off into the Netherworld.

"You're a part of our posse now?" I teased, surprised to hear a sharp edge in my tone. I immediately regretted it, even before a guarded mask fell over her features.

Liam didn't look at me, but I knew his subvocalized growl was all for me.

"Where else am I supposed to go?" Sera replied, her voice a low mumble.

I let out a long breath. It wasn't Sera's fault she got stuck here with us. I should really cut her some slack. Yeah. I planned to. Most likely. Right after I figured out her secrets.

"There," Liam said, pointing at a switchback a few hundred feet below us. "It's black, and a there's a few of them."

I watched the creatures, unable to identify their species. All I could see were amorphous shapes with purposeful movements. Movements in our direction.

Caden nodded. "I can't make out what they are, but they're black like the river."

We all turned to Sera, whose pallor had grown pale. She rushed over to look down at the black creatures.

"What the hells?" she said, roughly combing her fingers through her hair. "Crap. I must have transformed the water? Or maybe I released something out of the river?"

I blinked a few times, trying to make sense out of Sera's words. "You don't know what happened?"

She shrugged, a timid half-smile playing across her face.

"It's your magic. How can you not know?" I blurted out, my words louder than I intended.

"I just don't, okay?" Sera crossed her arms, hugging her midsection. "My magic has never been what you would call reliable. Sometimes when it kicks in, things go a little sideways."

"But they pulled you from Goldenbriar because you needed private tutoring," I replied, my mind putting together the puzzle pieces as the words flowed out of me. "You needed the tutor not because you were exceptional, but because you weren't good enough?"

Sera sighed, tapping her index finger on her nose. "I'm a powerful mage, but my magic is unstable. Volatile. So I've learned to keep my powers locked down and unused, lest things go haywire. But I felt like I had to fight off the ghouls to save Marcos from the river. I had to act, despite the danger."

Sera's revelation hit me like a slap to the face. She'd lied? Surprised at the depth of my reaction, I took a step back. Did I really have a right to feel betrayed by her evasion? But no, examining my feelings, I realized that wasn't the entirety of my upset. Caden's raised brows were his textbook 'I did not see that one coming' look, but watching Liam's and Marcos' expressions, I realized this wasn't news to them.

That awareness cut me to the bone.

"How could you two keep this from me? From us?" I demanded of Marcos and Liam. "Bros before mages, right?"

"It's Sera's business to disclose as she sees fit," Liam replied, his eyes still on the trail below us. "I trust her."

"That's your damned fated mates delusion speaking, Liam," I said. "You owe it to the rest of us to clue us in on threats."

His jaw ticked, and I could swear I heard a joint pop somewhere along Liam's tense frame. "It's no delusion. If I'd thought you were in danger, I would have spoken up. Sera's no threat to us."

Was he daft? Sera had just admitted to her powers

being erratic, and Liam somehow thought we'd be immune to the side effects?

I scanned the hillside below us, watching the blacker than black creatures resolutely making their way up the hill toward us.

"So Sera can't hurt us? Sure, okay, let's go with that. What about those creatures from the demon river down there? Are we immune to them too?" I couldn't help baiting him. Liam needed to understand how crazy he was sounding.

Liam spun to face me, his anger right at the surface. Caden pushed in between us, a hand on each of our chests, forcing us to keep our distance.

"Let's all agree we should have handled this sooner and with better finesse," Caden said. "Further, let's agree to get the fuck over it and figure out what to do about the wraiths. Right now we need to get moving and form a plan."

As much as I wanted satisfaction, I couldn't argue with Caden's logic. I looked him over, seeing the incubus with fresh eyes. This wasn't his style, but I approved. Perhaps the reality of risking his legacy had inspired him to turn over a new leaf?

"Agreed," I said. I held Liam's gaze, raising a brow.

Liam relented, but only a smidge. "Fine. I also agree," he said, but I could tell this conversation wasn't over.

Caden let go of us, and we both took a step back. I turned to Sera, strode over to her, and hooked my index finger under her chin. She stood defiantly, her arms crossed in front of her. Sera stared up at me. The depths of her brown eyes, the fire in her heart, and the curve of her full lips stirred something within me.

For a moment, I lost myself, imagining what it would be like to have her compliant under my touch. My gifts, when unleashed, could turn the meek ferocious, and the powerful submissive. Was Sera the type of woman who, when under my thrall, would raze the countryside? Or was she the type who'd purr like a kitten?

I wanted to find out.

But not now. Now, I needed to set expectations with our wee mage. "Do you promise you won't withhold anything from us again? Promise to share anything that impacts our safety?"

She held up her left hand with the palm towards me, the middle three fingers straight, and the thumb crossed over her pinky. "I solemnly swear I will disclose all pertinent knowledge to the posse."

I frowned, but then nodded my acceptance. I stepped away, breaking contact with Sera, feeling the loss of her touch acutely. "Perhaps if we hurry, we can outrun them."

"They've followed us for a while. Maybe they're tracking us using scent or magic?" Liam asked, glancing at Caden and Sera for confirmation.

"I don't know about either," Sera replied. She turned and walked away, gesturing for us to follow. "Come with me. There's something you need to see, and I have an idea."

A TRUST EXERCISE

FRANC

I and the others followed Sera across the small plateau we'd reached over to where she'd been wandering around earlier. There was a rock wall on our left and boulders on our right, blocking the view upward along the path. The flat section progressively narrowed until only one of us could pass at a time, but it soon became clear that this section of the trail was no trail at all. The slender route was only inches wide in sections, with the rock wall on one side and a sheer drop off on the other.

I rubbed the back of my head and shrugged my shoulders against the weight of my pack. "You've got to be kidding me."

Despite my comment, Marcos, who'd been uncommonly quiet, was already going through his pack and pulling out the rope.

"The map marks it as a traverse," Caden said. "But I feel the term doesn't fully qualify the death-trap nature of this crossing."

Sera pointed to the sheer wall as she talked. "After about fifteen or twenty feet, it looks like the trail widens again. If we use the rope in Marcos' pack and tie ourselves together, I bet we can get across safely. Sure, the footing is tricky, but the rock looks pocked, so handholds should be workable. But once we're over to the other side, it should be easier to defend ourselves from whatever those wraith creatures are."

Liam nodded at her, apparently sold on the idea. "That's clever. If we're lucky, they'll fall when they try to follow us over." He turned to Marcos. "Hand me the rope?"

"It's a simple party strategy, but thanks," Sera smiled up at him.

Liam took one end of the rope and knotted it around his waist. When he finished, he tied Sera in next, and then Marcos. Each of them had about eight to ten feet of slack between them.

When he approached me, I balked, holding up my hands. "We're just going to try this? No discussion of other alternatives?"

"It's the path to the Anzu, so we'll need to go that way anyway," Caden replied. "Unless we can find a way around, but I don't think any of us want to search for alternate routes with the wraiths closing in on us."

"Fine, then. Fine." I allowed Liam to tie the rope around my waist, wondering how things had gone south so quickly.

Oh, right. Hell.

Liam finished with Caden moments later and then led the way to the mouth of the traverse. Looking down into the ravine below, I felt less sure of this course of action.

"How is this supposed to work again?" I asked.

"It's simple," Liam replied. "If one of us slips…"

"The others all follow them to their doom?" I replied.

"No," Liam replied. "We catch whomever falls and pull them back up. We work as a team. Together, as we're meant to be."

I had to bite my tongue to avoid quipping back about Liam's crazy fated mates theory. Together, my ass.

Liam headed out onto the traverse, bravely stepping out, going hand over hand, his chest pressed across the wall. He turned back to Sera. "Only two of us on the wall at once. The third starts when I get across. Understood?"

"Understood," Marcos replied.

I adjusted my pack while I awaited my turn, making sure the straps were all flat and tight. "I hate everything about this."

"Weren't you lamenting last week that the posse never gets any quality time together?" Marcos replied, a weak smile pulling at the corners of his lips.

"I meant we needed more time carousing, partying, and fucking beautiful people together. Laughing over the good old days. Not whatever this bleak adventure is turning into."

My comment had drawn Sera's attention away from watching Liam's crossing. When her gaze met mine, I knew she was thinking back to the shed on the pixie reserve. Her cheeks flushed, and she looked away, focusing instead on Liam's forward movement.

Liam called back to us every few movements. "The footing is covered in scrabble. Step into the wall pocket above instead." He moves a couple of inches. "Right here there's a nice deep and smooth handhold."

When the rope ran out of slack between them, Sera

fearlessly stepped out onto the narrow strip, mimicking the movements Liam had made moments before. Their motions blurred into a series of punctuated landmarks across the difficult terrain. As Liam reached the far side, he shucked his backpack to the ground. He braced his body against a boulder, wrapping the rope around it, before motioning for Marcos to start his crossing. But when Marcos stepped up and shuffled across the traverse, the slight wobble in his movements set off alarm bells in my mind.

I couldn't remember a time that Marcos had looked shaken or weak. He must have been more badly hurt back at the river more badly than I'd realized.

"You okay, Marcos?" I asked.

"I'll be fine," he said. But if so, why was he shaky, with fresh sweat beading across his brow?

"You don't look fine." What could I do? If he fell, sure we could catch him, but preventing the fall would be preferable. "Can I please boost you?"

Marcos' gaze settled on me, a frown creasing his already perpetually serious expression. I knew he understood my euphemism for the gift of my power. "Your 'boosts' have consequences, Franc. I don't need to be drunk on your madness."

Marcos had seen my gift in action plenty of times. The power of Dionysos could obliterate a man's fear, unleashing the animal within, giving them the strength of many men, or, in this case, many shifters. Nightly at my club Velvet, supplicants, worshippers of the divine madness, would seek me and my gifts. They sought a temporary release from the mundane and the exhaustion of the daily grind. With a quick blessing from my powers, those lucky few could dance all night, bound in an ecstatic trance.

It didn't always go well, which I knew he'd seen for himself. When I touched some with my powers, they'd devolve into madness or a wild hunger for the flesh, but that was a rare thing. Now, with each wobbly step Marcos took, my fear for him grew. I noted he hadn't said no outright.

"Is everything okay?" Liam called out from the other side.

"I can make it," Marcos called back, but I heard the fear in his voice. "I've been dragging since falling into the river."

"I've noticed. We'll figure out a place to rest soon. But right now, we have to get across this traverse. I can go light with my push and we can manage the fallout," I reassured him. Sera hadn't yet reached the other side, but I worked my way out onto the ledge, following in the movements Liam and Sera had discovered along the way, intent on reaching Marcos before he slipped. "Do you agree?"

If the headstrong panther shifter didn't accept my help, I wasn't sure what I would do. Marcos was moving so slowly, I easily caught up to him. When his foot slipped on the scrabble beneath his shoes, I was close enough to grab him by the backpack, pulling his weight back against the wall.

We both panted from the exertion and stress of the near-fall, and me from rushing across the wall. Marcos' skin was pale and sweat poured off of him. I feared what would happen if I let go of his pack. I leaned closer, getting up in his face. I had to get through to him, or we might not be so lucky the next time. "Just a little boost, enough to fill you with the divine fire to keep you going."

Marcos nodded. "Yeah. Just a little. I don't know why I'm so exhausted."

I sighed with relief. "We'll figure it out, but in the meantime, here you go." I kept my hand firm on his backpack and leaned closer, pressing my lips against his cheek. I said a silent prayer, an invocation of Dionysos, and a blessing to Marcos' body and mind. The power rushed through me, swirling around us like a sudden but brief tempest.

I pulled back, watching him closely. I'd aimed for a minimal effect, but everyone reacted to the madness of Dionysos differently. Marcos shuddered as the power washed over him. When he opened his eyes, they sparkled with a joy of life I felt mirrored in my very soul. "I've never let you do that before."

"There's a first time for everything." I could feel the power of my god's lineage surging through his veins. My power couldn't heal, but the consciousness shift was often profound, sometimes leading to a new way of viewing the world that lasted for some time. "Doesn't have to be the last, either. How are you feeling?"

He flexed his arms, a self-assured smile spreading across his face. Already his pallor had improved. "Like I could run up a mountain?"

I smiled. "There's time for that later. For now, let's just get across this ledge."

"Oh yeah, right?" He looked around us with fresh eyes, as if unaware of where he was or the situation we were in. But when he adjusted his holds on the wall, it was with a surety he'd lacked a few moments before. I released his backpack, but stayed close to him as we worked our way across together.

I kept my attention on Marcos as I watched the others. Caden followed close behind me, no doubt not wanting to be left on the far side when the wraiths arrived at the top of the pass. There were a few tense, silent moments passed with only the sounds of our scrabbling and heavy breathing.

When Marcos stepped off the far side of the ledge and joined Sera and Liam on the far platform, I finally relaxed. Marcos swept Sera up, holding her tight in his arms, his face buried in her neck. Sera loosened the rope from around Marcos' waist. Freed from the constraint, he walked her over to the rock wall, pressing her against it as he ran his nose repeatedly from her face to her shoulders.

From Sera's appreciative whimpers, she wasn't minding the attention one bit.

I joined them a few moves later. Happy to be out of the danger zone, at least for this most recent hurdle the Netherworld had thrown at us. I glanced back at Caden, who appeared to be making his way with a fair amount of skill. I pulled the slack out of the line as he moved closer, intent on helping him too, if needed, but it didn't look like he'd need the help.

"You boosted Marcos?" Liam asked me. He had been winding our rope around the boulder as we'd reached the other side, keeping the lax excess to a minimum.

I nodded. "He looked shaky. I figured a small boost would help get him through the current crisis. Looks like he's in the 'cuddle and hug' stage."

Liam frowned. "He's likely to crash later, but it was good thinking."

"He was more badly hurt in the demon river episode than I realized. We need to find another place to rest that's safe to give him some time to heal up."

Liam's grim smile echoed my concerns that we'd be able to find something safe in this landscape.

"I'm glad you're okay, and I appreciate the affection, but you can put me down, Marcos," Sera said.

Marcos "I never want to put you down, little mage. I want to lose myself in you until I can't remember what day it is anymore."

"I'm confident you've already lost track of the time," Liam said, shaking his head. "How long will his god-drunk episode last?" he asked me.

"Maybe a couple of hours?"

Caden had almost reached our side, and I held out a hand to him, helping to steady him as took the last step and joined. He got to work untying his rope, while Liam stood and coiled his end. I pulled off my backpack, stretching my shoulders after hauling it around all day long.

Marcos groaned, still leaning against Sera. "I want to dive right in into you and taste every inch of your skin. I want your scent all over me and mine all over you."

Sera flashed Marcos a sultry smile. "Do you?" she said, arching her brow. She took his face in her hands, forcing him to look her in the eye. "How about we save that for later, okay champ?"

He growled, his hands gripping her ass in a proprietary fashion.

"You're such a big, powerful man. Can you help me help the boys?"

"Anything for you," Marcos rumbled.

I rolled my eyes. "Shifters, am I right?" I said to Caden. "Sera doesn't seem to mind."

I heard movement from across the traverse and looked up to see one of the wraith creatures had finally caught up to us. It wandered around the plateau for a few moments and then stopped moving. It had no eyes that I could see, but I felt the weight of its focus fall upon us. It moved like a phantom on the wind, a cluster of shadowy night tied together by will alone.

"Now what?" Caden asked, voicing what the rest of us were thinking.

"We wait and see if it can cross the traverse," Liam explained. "I'd recommend we leave and put some distance between us just in case."

I watched as the wraith approached the edge of the drop off, and then hesitated. I'd seen more than one following us. Even if this one didn't make it over, would the next brave the journey?

"No," I said, planting my hands on my hips. "I've had enough."

"We're all over this," Sera said, coming to stand beside me. Marcos was right behind her, but he stood there quietly, running his fingers down her back. "But what options do we have?"

"It's been one thing after another here. At this pace, I doubt we'll all make it through this challenge, much less another four. We need to renegotiate."

"With the wraith?" Liam asked.

"Of course not," I replied. Resolved, I spoke the three magic words. "Taneisha. Taneisha. Taneisha."

A moment passed, and then two. Then the fae's melodious voice broke the silence, "Hey, if it isn't my favorite doomed posse." We spun around to discover Tink standing there, resplendent in a midnight blue sheath dress, her platinum blonde hair pulled back and plaited ornately, hanging down over her bare shoulder. She wrinkled her little button nose at us as she frowned. "Just kidding, haters." She looked around, assessing the situation. "I don't understand. Why'd you call on me, arrogant god of madness? I don't see any legacy."

The fae appeared so dainty and harmless, in complete juxtaposition to the position of power she wielded over us. I wanted to scream in frustration, but I held my temper.

"I was hoping we could talk," I said.

She arched an imperious brow. "Talk? The time for talking is long past."

Sera reached out and touched my hand, but her gaze was on Taneisha. "We request parley."

Tink blinked a few times, and then laughed. "What, you're pirates now?"

I had no idea where Sera had pulled out that idea. I'd intended to demand the fae be reasonable, but I would let Sera play this out first.

Sera crossed her arms over her chest. "You're refusing to honor parley?"

Tink looked from Sera to the rest of us, still laughing. "Seriously?"

We were all tired, worn out, and over her shit, so no one responded to the fae. Instead, we all watched and waited, unified in our need for a win, any win, against our capricious foe.

She sobered up and crossed her arms, mimicking Sera's body language. "Fine then, this should be good. I'll parley, pirate posse. Have at it, mage."

Sera took a deep breath. A scrabbling sound came from behind us. Turning around, I saw a wraith crossing the traverse. My heart skipped a beat, knowing we had only minutes left before it reached us.

Taneisha sighed, exasperated. "Hold on," she said, waving her hand for us to move and then threading her way between us to the ledge. She held her hand up, forming an O with her thumb and forefinger, and blew through the ring. A series of bright pink bubbles emerged from the other side like a bubble gun on maximum blast, floating through the air towards the wraith. Then she turned and walked back toward us, taking a seat on the boulder Liam had used earlier, watching us expectantly. "So, what did you have in mind to negotiate?"

Behind her, the magical pink bubbles reached the wraith, popping on impact. The curious effect was totally silent, but looked like a series of explosions across its surface. In seconds, the wraith had dissipated into a fine ash, which drifted off on the breeze away from us.

At least that was one less problem on our proverbial plate.

Sera glanced my way, and I nodded for her to continue. Taneisha didn't hate her, after all. She'd already handled the wraith without our having to beg for it, so I wasn't sure what else to ask for.

"You gave us these awesome supplies and set us up with useful things like the rope, clothes, food ,and water. Even the map. We're super grateful for all of that forethought. But I have to know, is your intention to kill us?" Sera asked.

Taneisha tilted her head to the side, pursing her lips. Did she actually not know, or was she fucking with us?

"You're very welcome, and I don't think so? I mean, maybe?" She shrugged her shoulders. "Just a little?"

"Could we get your assurance that none of us will die?" Sera pressed.

"Oh," Taneisha frowned. "You mean all of you? Yeah, I don't know if I can promise that."

I sighed. Maybe Tink was a psychopath?

"But, you like me, right?" Sera asked.

Taneisha smiled. "I like you plenty, you clever and funny girl, but get to your point."

"Okay. Do you want me to die?"

"No, of course not."

"I'm relieved to hear it. Would you grant me a teeny, tiny, boon?"

Taneisha crossed her arms again, her brow furrowing. "Maybe? What do you want?"

"I need a safe place to sleep and rest before we deal with the Anzu. I'm not asking to put off the showdown or otherwise skirt your rules. I figure, just like you gave us those handy backpacks, you could throw in some shelter. Could you make that happen?"

"I can do anything I like," she snapped back. Taneisha bounced her foot, tapping her barefoot toes against the ground. "But like, you'd take them with you, right? If I help you, and it benefits the posse... Well, do you see my conflict?"

She said that as if we weren't even here, listening to every word they said.

Sera shrugged, as if her plans shouldn't even matter to the fae. We all knew making the posse suffer was at the forefront of Taneisha's mind, so of course it mattered.

Taneisha leaned forward and whispered

conspiratorially. Again, as if we all couldn't hear her. "You sure you wouldn't prefer I whisk you away from these boneheads? I bet Pepper is missing you back at the coffee house. In an instant you could be free of the Netherworld. Free of my trials. Free of the posse."

No way in hell was I letting Tink take Sera away.

Wait a minute. I shook my head to clear my thoughts. The last thing I wanted was for Sera to take Tink up on her offer, but the strength of my reaction surprised me. Taneisha returning Sera to her normal life would be a great deal for the mage, who hadn't deserved to get drawn into our drama. But without the mage here, surely things would go less well for us with the fae.

I didn't doubt I was being selfish. I'd been accused of being an unrepentant narcissist, only up for partying more than once. An image of Sera staring up at me, promising to be open with those deep brown eyes and full, kissable lips, came unbidden to my mind. Then I remembered waking up next to her, my erection pressed against the soft, inviting curve of her ass as she mewled and ground against Caden. Of course, I didn't want her taken away, and not just because it would help my brothers and I with Taneisha.

I glanced around at my brothers of choice, all of whom remained silent, no doubt as fearful as I was of unintentionally goading an outburst from Taneisha. An irate fire burned in Liam's eyes. Marcos' fists were clenched, his jaw grinding audibly. Caden's expression was dark and stormy. I didn't know about my brothers and I being fated mates with the mage, but I was sure none of us were willing to let her go. Not yet. Maybe not ever.

For her part, Sera's face was a blank canvas. "Your offer

to take me home is generous, Taneisha, but I'm not ready to go quite yet. That's why I asked for the boon."

The fae's nostrils flared, but otherwise she kept her composure. Taneisha stood up and walked over to Sera, reaching out to tuck the mage's hair behind her ear in an overly familiar gesture. My pulse sped up, aware that at any moment, the fae might disappear with Sera or do any of a million unexpected or random things which were pretty much out of my control.

"You want to stay with them?" Taneisha asked Sera. "But you agree they're insufferable, right?"

Sera's easy smile was followed up by a grunting laugh. "They totally are. Impossible at times, even. Often also tedious."

Taneisha chuckled. "Yeah, right? I'll admit they're hot. Maybe you just need more time to get this childhood attraction out of your system?"

"It's cheaper than therapy."

Taneisha burst into laughter, and Sera followed along a minute later. I didn't even know what I was witnessing or how to process it. Did Sera just imply flirting with us was her way of working out her sexual angst from our days at Goldenbriar Academy?

So why was that admission somehow also a turn on? Ways I could help her work out that angst flashed through my head, many of them involving her lips around my cock, or her gasping as I thrust myself deep into her core. But wait, hadn't she joked about her attraction to our posse before? Had that not been a joke? Liam and Marcos were convinced she was their fated mate. Our fated mate. Were we just a fun fantasy for her? Something to work out and move on from?

I saw a million ways this could go poorly for my brothers and I. I didn't want them, or myself, getting hurt by anyone's games. Not even a supposed fated mate.

When Taneisha recovered from her laughing fit, she held up a hand. A little floating ball of light appeared nestled in her palm, glowing with pale intensity. She took Sera's hand and poured the ball of light into her palm, where it glowed and pulsed.

"I grant you your boon, Sera. Take this will o' wisp, who will lead you to safe harbor. Mind you, I will ask you for recompense at an appropriate time, and I will not be denied. Good luck with your therapy, sister."

"Thank you for your indulgence," Sera replied, cradling the ball of wisp between her palms.

Taneisha disappeared, leaving all of us on the hillside. The will o' wisp rose up into the air, carried on an unseen wind. It floated ahead of us along the trail upward, it's speed easy enough to match.

"I'd advise you to keep up," Sera called back over her shoulder, attention focused on our new guide.

As if that was ever in doubt.

CHEAPER THAN THERAPY

SERA

I walked ahead of the guys, feeling their attention on me the entire way. None of them spoke, and I didn't bother looking back. I heard them and knew they'd follow.

No doubt I'd bruised their egos from the conversation I'd had with Taneisha, but they would just have to get over it. I'd said and done what I needed to do to get us all to safety for the night, and if they couldn't understand that, then they could take a flying leap for all I cared.

Except I cared much more than I'd wanted to admit. When Taneisha had offered to send me back home, my heart had leapt at the chance to return to the safety of my ordinary life filled with pastries and foamy lattes. But returning to that safety also meant leaving the posse to fend for themselves against the wily fae. Not to mention also giving up on my brief journey into the lands of adventure with fellow supes. The image had left my stomach in somersaults. Sure, they were all adults, and they'd certainly earned their conflict with the fae, but I knew my presence gave them an edge.

Plus, I didn't want to leave them. I knew it wasn't just because I thought they needed me, which they mostly did. I needed them, too. I didn't understand fully why yet, but my heart knew it to be true.

The will o' wisp had been floating back and forth over the trail until it suddenly veered downhill. I clambered over boulders and around the scrub brush to follow it. The wisp graciously waited for me when I fell behind. I heard the guys following behind after me, but I didn't dare look back in case I lost sight of the wisp. A few minutes later down the hill, it led me unerringly to a door in the hillside which hadn't been visible from the trail above.

The plain, wooden door, shaped like a broad leaf and the color of dirt. was hidden behind a stand of bushes. I tried the handle, which was locked. The wisp, which had been floating around my head and shoulders, shot towards the handle after I'd let go of it, disappearing into the locking mechanism. A distinctive click came from the lock, and when I retried the door, it opened to reveal a dark room beyond.

I tried not to worry about what Taneisha would demand for this boon, but the thought itched at the back of my mind.

"Would you like me to go in first?" Liam, who'd caught up with me, offered.

Marcos was slowly catching up, still favoring his right leg. Whatever boost Franc had given him earlier, it was fading fast. I saw Franc and Caden walking behind him, speaking to each other in low tones.

"No. I don't imagine the fae would agree to a boon just to hide a monster inside."

The warmth in Liam's smile tugged at my heart. "I agree. A surprise monster would be pedestrian by her standards." He placed a hand on my shoulder, and I melted into the comfort of his touch. "Just to say it, whatever Taneisha extracts for her price, I'll be there to help. All of us will be."

"You can't speak for all of them, Liam, but I appreciate you backing me up."

"They'll come around."

I frowned, but didn't feel like arguing with him. Liam and Marcos' wild insistence that the entire posse were all mated to me wasn't something the others agreed with. Heck, it wasn't something I'd bought into either. There was no magical promise that things would all work out or that everyone would come around.

Not that I needed or wanted them to. Sure, I'd like a partner to spend my life with, but I wasn't looking for a mate. Certainly not multiple mates. I sighed. So why hadn't I taken Taneisha up on her offer to send me back home? Oh yeah, because despite the danger and the sometimes temperamental demi-gods, I was having fun.

Imagine that.

Taneisha had joked that I needed time to work out my childhood attractions. Was that all this was? If so, was that bad? Was there any harm in enjoying the time together?

I steeled my nerves, pulled the door open wide, and entered the cave, relieved to have the safety of this simple, wooden door separating us from the wilds of the Netherworld, if only for one night.

Liam followed me in, sweeping his flashlight around

the space. Near the door was a gas lamp, which he set to lighting while I held his flashlight. Once it was going, the dim lamplight illuminated the space which held a pair of couches framing a central fireplace. Off to one side was a tiny kitchenette with a sink, cupboard, and a small table with a couple more lamps. There weren't any decorations or personal items lying around. When Liam turned up the lamp, four doors on the far wall came into view, all of them open to the rooms beyond.

"We should search those rooms and make sure this place is empty," Franc said, startling me as he brushed past me. I'd been so absorbed in taking in this secret shelter, I hadn't realized the others had come in behind us.

"I'll help," Liam said, following Franc towards the back.

Caden shut the door behind us, throwing the bolt. "Does it look like someone lives here?"

Marcos brushed his fingers over the table and then rubbed his fingers together. "Not recently, if this dust is any sign."

"I wonder if there are many hideouts like this?" I asked.

"Some demons prefer living here over the earth plane, but a few stay here year round," Caden explained, walking around the couches. He cleared the extra lamps off of the table, sat on a couch, and pulled the map out, spreading it open across the table. "At least that's what I've been told. This reads like more of a hunting cabin."

"Hunting?" I asked, not really expecting a response. "I can pretty easily imagine a few extreme hunting options for Netherworld visitors."

Liam emerged from one room. "That explains how

austere everything is. The owners intended this hideaway for short-term use only. This room one has a pair of beds." He stuck his head in the next one. "Same here. Not much else."

Franc came out of the next room. "More beds." He ducked into the last room on the right. "Oh, there's a bathroom with a walk-in shower in here."

"Shower? I call dibs," I said, sliding my backpack from my shoulders.

Franc flashed me a sly smile. "You're tiny and the shower's big enough to share. Aren't you a proponent of water conservation?"

An image of all five of us in the shower together flashed through my mind, heating my cheeks and ratcheting my internal temperature up a few degrees. "I doubt that would be a quick shower."

"Definitely not," Franc replied, his gaze lazily traveling over my curves. There was the barest hint of magic in the air. A tinge of sultry heat that promised so much potential.

I thought about his offer for a few seconds. Did I want Franc? Sure, I'd always been curious what the demi-god was like, and what it would be like to have all of that ecstatic potency aimed in my direction. I glanced around the room at the others. We'd shared a fun, intimate, and racy night back at the nature preserve together. Would dipping my toes a second time satiate my curiosity, or only open the door to more?

In a flash of boldness, I kind of wanted to know, even though I knew such affairs wouldn't be approved of by our families or supe society. Inter-species dating was one thing. Dating a handful of men? Quite another.

When I realized all of their expectant gazes were on me, I balked. "I think I need a little time to myself."

"Your loss," Franc whispered.

Where was a hand fan when you needed it?

For a demi-god of partying and madness, he really ran hot and cold. Compared to the shifters, who ran hot all the time. Even now both Marcos and Liam's watchful gazes followed me around the room, the unmistakable green and yellow flashes in their eyes reminding me of the beasts lying just below the surface.

"This waystation is a welcome respite, worthy of your boon," Liam said. "Why don't you go get cleaned up?"

I scooted off toward the bathroom, excited for not only the prospect of getting fully clean, but also for some private time to myself. Closing the door behind me, I discovered the large shower was certainly big enough for all of us, and the stack of towels on a nearby shelf were big enough to cover a small bed. Whoever designed this place must have expected the typical occupants to be quite large indeed. The bathroom was otherwise as spartan as the rest of the place, with a side room containing the toilet and a simple sunken sink in a counter with a mirror hung from the wall behind it.

When I turned on the water, the spray was strong, and the stream quickly heated. "Thank you, Taneisha," I whispered, wondering if she would hear me.

I stripped off my clothes, somewhat surprised at the level of grime covering my feet and ankles. When I stepped in under the water, the heat was such a welcome sensation I could have cried. I'd been so worn out from the trials of the day and the constant walking that my magic was silent, at least for the time being.

Thank the gods for small miracles.

There were a couple of bars of soap stacked on a ledge, and I tested them out. I found one that smelled of lavender and used it to lather and rinse my entire body twice over. On that same ledge were small jars, which I assumed were for hair care, but not all of them smelled promising. I took a guess with one that smelled of vanilla and honeysuckle and had a texture like conditioner, working that through my long locks.

While waiting for the conditioner to work its magic, I aimed the shower head at the space between my shoulders and zoned out for a while.

A tapping at the door roused me from my reverie. "Yeah?" I said, my mind snapping to attention, remembering the four supe men on the other side of that door.

The door swung open, and Franc stepped in, closing it behind him. His gaze held mine, his presence taking up considerable real estate in the bathroom, making me feel like he was standing right here beside me. "You look like you're enjoying yourself."

Somehow, I didn't feel at all self-conscious in front of the demi-god. Perhaps it had been the days in close quarters together? Or was it knowing he'd already seen me naked?

"I swear this hideaway is a pocket of paradise in hell," I said, rinsing the conditioner out of my hair.

His grin widened. "Are you planning to share this paradise or are you going to hoard all the hot water for yourself?"

"I'm no monster, Franc." I teased as I studied him leaning against the wall. "For a god of ecstasy, you're showing a lot of restraint right now." I scrubbed at my scalp with my fingertips, feeling the silky bubbling of the water cascade down my body and over my breasts, bobbing with every motion.

Franc was still as stone when he answered. "You can't force ecstasy, Sera. Much like a vampire, that aspect of my power must be invited in. Only those willing to surrender themselves can be filled with the madness of the gods."

Surrender myself? His arched brow left no question as to the nature of his invitation. I realized my mouth was gaping open, and I quickly snapped it shut, planting my hands on my hips. "That's a pretty long-winded and euphemism-filled way of saying you wanna bang."

A sly smirk played across Franc's lips as amusement lit up his sky-blue eyes. "My lineage is known for giving powerful performances and moving orations."

"Oh my gods, seriously?" I burst into laughter, unable to hold it back any longer. I didn't mind his over the top bravado. Instead, I found Franc's direct manner refreshing and a turn-on all on its own. "I'm the last person who needs more madness. My powers are dangerous enough. Can you imagine what could happen if I just let them run wild?"

"Maybe that's the problem?" he replied. "Have you ever tried unbottling the genie to see what happens?"

I bit my lip. Of course Franc was pushing to know more about my magical problems. "Back at Goldenbriar, there were accidents. I landed Professor Gauthier in the hospital my freshman year with a head injury. He'd been coaching me to tap into my powers and I summoned a whirlwind which picked him up and dumped him on his head."

His brows arched. "That was you?" he asked, and I nodded. Franc moved closer, leaning against the opening of the shower. "I remember hearing about Gauthier being out and the utter destruction of his training lab. He never seemed quite right in the head after that, but his injury wasn't your fault. The teachers all assume a level of risk helping students learn their powers."

"I still feel bad about it," I mumbled. "Since then, I've always been afraid of who I might hurt next."

"Then you've never experienced the full extent of what you're capable of?" Franc asked. His mask of bravado had dropped, revealing a sadness in his eyes that touched me.

I shook my head. "I'm too worried about losing control."

Franc stepped into the water, still wearing his pants and shirt, and cupped my face with his hand, brushing his thumb across my lower lip. My heart thrummed against my chest, the tension between us suddenly ramping up.

"You've been desperately holding tight to your control for years," he whispered, and then dipped his chin and looked up at me. "What I wouldn't give to see you come undone." His sky-blue eyes held my gaze, daring me to make the first move. To let him in. To surrender to the moment.

What the hell? Why shouldn't I? When I got back to my regular life, would I have opportunities like this again? Lacking the desire to resist, my resolve crumbled. I reached out, grabbing Franc by his soaked shirt collar, and pulled him against me.

His lips pressed against mine, hungry and urgent with need, pinning my body against the stone wall. His touch was rough, as if he was just barely able to channel his frenzied hunger. I opened to him with a ferocity I hadn't realized was lurking right beneath the surface. Was it a product of years of unfulfilled flirting? The tension of surviving through hell, chased by one danger after another? Or perhaps it was being stuck together with this band of brothers, knowing there was no way out but by working together?

Whatever the driving forces, I couldn't deny the animalistic hunger building within me. Although I enjoyed running Charmed Brews, peddling lattes and tabletop gaming day in and day out, there'd always been something missing. Franc's fervor, the heat of his lips, the feel of his hands exploring my body, and the press of his body against mine fed a hunger I hadn't known I had.

But now that I'd had a taste of Franc, I wanted more. I hadn't ever felt this insatiable before. Was it being surrounded by the posse constantly? Some supposed fae trick? Whatever the reasons, I could figure those out later. I needed more of Franc. Now.

While I'd been caught up in the intensity of our passion, Franc had shed his shirt. I dug my fingers into the corded, athletic muscles of his back, wondering when he found time to work out between running his club and partying.

Water rained down over us, the steamy water vapor cocooning us in a world all our own. Franc ran a line of greedy kisses down my neck, nibbling and biting along the way. His fingers found my nipple, rolling and pinching it as I ground myself against him, hungry for more. I ran my fingers down over his taut abdomen, finding and then tearing at the button of his waistband, hearing it hit the shower floor with a sharp ping.

I gasped. "Whoops! I didn't..."

Franc's kiss took my breath away, and for a moment I forgot what I'd been about to say. "You never have to apologize to me for your passion." He pulled back and unzipped his pants, revealing an impressive bulge hidden behind green boxers. "You wanted these off?" he teased.

"Yes. All of it," I replied, my mouth suddenly dry, despite being surrounded with water on all sides.

Franc reached into his pocket and pulled out a couple of condoms, placing them on the ledge behind my head.

"You don't suffer from a lack of confidence," I said. I would have given him more hell, but then he peeled off his wet pants and underwear. I couldn't take my eyes off of him. All of him. Oh, my. Were all demi-gods so well-endowed, or was Franc especially lucky?

"What? I figured someone might find them useful." He arched his brow.

I reached up and grabbed one packet and gently ripped it open. "Someone does." I held up the condom, feeling an anxious-edged smile tug at my lips. "You want to do the honors, or should I?"

He smirked, snatching the condom from my fingertips. "Happy to." Franc rolled the condom onto himself, watching my reaction more than his progress.

When he finished, Franc moved in close, and slid his hands over my ass. He picked me up, and I wrapped my legs around him. He slid the length of his cock against my pussy as the weight of his body pressed deliciously against mine. Franc caught my lips in a deep kiss while I squirmed against him, trying to find an angle that would deliver more than just a tease.

When we took a breather from the kiss, Franc

chuckled. He held still, his cock pressed against my folds, his body pinning mine in place against the wall. Water continued to pour over us, the only motion besides our breathing and the throbbing of my swollen clit.

"So we agree it's no fun when someone holds out?"

I laughed, hearing the breathy desire in my voice. "You're trying to teach me life lessons? Now?"

"Everyone's motivated differently. Is it working?" he asked, bucking against me.

I let out a low groan and then slid my hand down and under my thigh. I searched until I located his shaft, which I stroked and teased. "Maybe? It's weird foreplay. You're at risk of going off half-cocked."

"I do nothing halfway," he said, biting his lip. Then his expression suddenly turned serious. Vulnerable even. "I want to trust you, Sera, but first I need to know you'll tell me, well, all the posse, when your magic is off kilter. Will you tell us what's going on and what you need?"

My heart caught in my throat. Franc's emotions were right there on the surface and all I wanted in that moment was to reassure him. "I'll tell you, and the others, I swear it." I took a deep breath, trying to clear the surprise tears threatening the edges of my vision. "I could have left when I had the chance, but I'm here for you. All of you."

I didn't consider myself the best at giving speeches, but my words were enough to urge Franc into action. He shifted position and thrust up into me, his kisses capturing my groans of pleasure and chasing away my storm-cloud thoughts. He moved slowly at first as I adjusted to his size, waiting until I was digging my fingers into his hips, urging him on.

When at last Franc wrung an orgasm out of me, I could

barely breathe as my mind shattered into a million pieces. He slowed down then, clearly not yet done himself yet, allowing me a few moments to recover. I sighed against his shoulder, feeling more in balance than I had in days. Months? Years?

I would have tried having sex every day before this quest, had I such available, encouraging, and enthusiastic partners. I couldn't deny something was definitely off, newly off, with my magic. It seemed both more and less chaotic than before, but I did not know what had changed to make it so. I needed to figure it out, but now I had better things to focus on, like the demi-god rocking his substantial cock slowly in and out of me.

When I opened my eyes, to my surprise, I saw Caden had slipped into the room. He stood silent, drinking in the sight of pleasure as only an incubus could. Franc glanced behind us, holding Caden's gaze for a moment before returning his attention to me.

Caden seemed content to watch, but I wanted more of him. I gestured for him to come over and join us.

He shrugged, his short, black, messy hair hanging down into his sky-blue eyes. "I'm afraid I get drawn like a moth to sexual energy. I didn't mean to intrude." Only an incubus could look so contrite and sexy at the same time.

"Get over yourself and come over here," I said, feeling more than thinking my way through the present situation.

I didn't miss the heated gleam in Franc's eyes. "Yes, brother, join us."

THAT'S HOW THE RESOLVE CRUMBLES

CADEN

I didn't have to be asked twice.

Franc and Sera's sensual energy had drawn me into the bathroom. The irresistible scent of sex on the air was not to be denied. Knowing who and where those nearby were having sex was a blessing and a curse, especially since nearby included a pretty broad range. I didn't like to intrude where I wasn't welcome, which left me with a lot of frustrated fantasies.

Like this morning. Except I didn't want to get entangled with Sera. I kept everyone at a distance, even Franc, who knew me best of all and knew most of my secrets. If I couldn't keep my distance, I didn't trust myself to keep my carefully designed charade in place from Sera and the rest of the posse on this journey.

I knew Sera wanted me. She'd made that abundantly clear earlier. Not taking her and Franc up on their offer at the time had taken almost all of my resolve. Now, watching Franc's delectably naked backside as he slowly pumped into Sera's pussy while she watched me over his shoulder with that come-hither look, I was undone.

My best intentions slid right down that drain. I was strong, even for an incubus, but I was powerless to refuse the combination of Sera's siren call and my longtime lover, Franc's invitation. I walked into the shower and peeled off my clothes, sighing with relief as I freed my erection from the constriction of the leather pants. I left my necklace on, otherwise I would have drawn Liam and Marcos into the mix, and that wasn't what I had in mind for tonight.

I'd never liked the idea of coercing someone into my arms with my powers. Where was the fun of using an enchantment few could withstand? Amping up the enjoyment once they were interested? Most definitely.

I clenched my jaw, feeling my molars protest my grinding. I needed to keep some measure of distance between Sera and I. I had to. I would not be foolish like those mating-driven shifters, and I didn't believe demons had fated mates. Especially me, an incubus? Can you imagine? Stuck with one woman? One... anyone? Anything?

Not gonna happen. In my experience, no one was that interesting for that long, and I had a ravenous hunger to keep up with.

Perhaps I should have walked right out of the room, but I needed a taste. Just a taste, I repeated to myself, but my cock twitched with anticipation of so much more.

I approached them, squaring myself up behind Franc, but then took a moment to drink him, well, both of them, in. I loved everything about Franc. He was my partner in crime, confidant, best friend, and he had the literal body of a Greek god, so I had to take a moment to appreciate the living sculpture that he represented. I could look at those muscular shoulders, defined back, and the most perfect ass sporting pert, round globes with a pair of dimples on either side of his sacrum.

Sheer perfection.

Sera, I knew, but not at all well. Spending the past couple of days with her had left me with more questions than answers. I appreciated her sexual appetite, something no woman should ever feel ashamed of. I respected that she asked for what she wanted. How could I not?

Franc cast me a glance over his shoulder. "What are you waiting for back there?"

"I'm sure I don't know," I drawled. I took hold of his hips and pressed into him slowly, giving Franc time to accommodate my size. His groan of pleasure almost undid me and I had to close my eyes to mute the intensity of the moment and control myself.

Sera grabbed me by the back of my neck, pulling me in for a long kiss. She nibbled my lower lip, then flicked her tongue against mine. I opened my eyes to see a moment of confusion, followed by recognition, passed over her features as she realized I had a tongue piercing. No doubt she was wondering how that might feel used in more sensitive areas.

Not today, you little minx! I longed to tease her clit with my piercing. Would that be novel for her? I drove into Franc, directing how he ground against Sera. I felt like I was fucking both of them at once, as I set the pacing.

"More," Sera begged, and I delivered, speeding up. "Yes. Incredible." Sera had been reduced to one-word sentences. "I'm. Coming." Her orgasm caused a cascade reaction, sending Franc over the edge, and feeling the force of his release, I came a moment later.

FULL DISCLOSURE

SERA

I was glowing all over, lips raw from Caden's and Francs kisses and pussy still throbbing from what might have been the hottest sex ever. Or so far?

I chuckled to myself. If things kept going in this direction, I might not be able to walk in a couple of days. A tightness clamped down on my heart, as I realized the next few days might be all I had before returning to my regular life. Which was definitely, of course, what I still wanted. At least I thought so?

Caden pulled away from Franc, abruptly going to stand under the water streaming from the shower head. In my gut I knew something was off, and a glance at Franc's troubled expression confirmed my fears.

Franc gently kissed me on the forehead, and then pulled me away from the wall, holding me by my ass as I lowered my feet to the ground. He didn't let go until I steadied myself, both of our attentions focused on the incubus.

"Is everything okay, Caden?" Franc asked.

The demon sped through his shower, taking his time before answering. A moment ago he'd been lost to pleasure along with Franc and I, but now he was all business. As much as I wanted to revel in our post-sex high, supporting Caden and his quest took priority.

Caden soaped himself up and then rinsed off under the hot water before he turned toward us. "It's not. I keep pretending everything's fine, but I just can't anymore. I need to get everyone together to go over my plan."

"You know we're all here to help you," I said. "Do you mean a plan to get back your legacy from the Anzu?" I stepped out of the shower and dried off before slipping into a change of clothes.

He nodded, wrapping a towel around his middle, which on him was downright indecent. "Before I came in here, I was studying the map. I know what we need to do to defeat the monster."

A couple of minutes later, the shower was off and we were all seated on the couches with the Netherworld map laid out on the table between us. Well, everyone but Caden, who paced back and forth at one end of the couches. I'd sat down next to Liam, while Marcos and Franc sat across from us.

I was certain both Liam and Marcos knew what had gone down in the shower, more or less. Liam had a contented smile, as if everything was going to plan. I supposed it made sense because the wolf was convinced we were all fated to be together, however improbable that reality was. Marcos, however, looked sullen and out of sorts, his frown a clear sign of his discomfort. Was he upset because he didn't trust Caden, still in pain from the injury to his leg earlier, or disappointed because we had left him out? A little of everything?

I wanted to find out what was up with Marcos, but Caden's pacing drew all of my attention.

"What's the plan?" I asked.

Caden stopped in his tracks, a frenetic edge to his movements. "The plan? Yes." He hesitated a moment, as if not sure where to begin. "Okay, yes." He knelt down in front of the table, pointing his finger at the map. "This is where we are now. The path we've been following has brought us super close to the Anzu's nesting grounds." He pointed to a spot showing a nest on a spire.

"That's not the actual spire, right?" Liam asked,

"No, but we're in the shadow of it," Caden replied. "I'd guess we could get there in under an hour, tops."

"Any ideas on how we get the seeds from the Anzu when we get there?" I asked.

Caden ran a hand through his hair, tugging the wet strands away from his face. "A beast that size has to hunt to eat. I say we sneak up on its nest, wait until it flies away, and then find the seeds and run before it gets back."

"What if the bird-man doesn't hunt every day?" Marcos asked. "How long do you figure we hide and wait?"

Caden shrugged. "If the Anzu doesn't leave, then we go with Plan B. We start a fire to distract it and then steal the seeds."

I had an idea who'd be starting the fire in that scenario, which was fine with me. "What if that doesn't make it back off? Do we fight it?" I heard the words leave my lips, surprised to feel a rush of excitement coursing through my veins.

"Only as a last resort," Caden replied. "Even working

together, we may not be strong enough to take him out. The last thing I want is for any of you to get hurt."

"I don't like it," Liam said. He leaned forward, pouring over the map as if he might discover something Caden had missed. "This situation could get out of hand. Quickly." He looked at me, and I heard his unspoken subtext. Liam thought of me as his, well their, mate. I'm sure the very last thing he wanted to do was risk me to get back some seeds.

"That's why aiming for minimal interaction is the key," Caden replied.

"I think I've proven I can hold my own," I said, feeling my back straighten.

"You certainly have, little mage. I'd rather face the beast head on, but Caden's idea to start with the least confrontational option is sound," Franc replied. "If that doesn't work, we can always fall back on your enchantments."

Marcos huffed out a breath. "We shouldn't put Sera in that position. She's already been using her powers at every turn to help us out. And for what? Some old seeds?"

Caden's eyes flashed red, but he held his tongue. Franc sat forward, elbows on his knees, and sighed in frustration. "I won't have you disparaging Caden's legacy. You can't know the depth of meaning in someone else's heart."

"Okay, but I have a right to understand what they're about, right?" Marcos said to Franc, and then looked at Caden. "I think we all have a right to know what we're risking life and limb tomorrow for."

There was a tense, silent moment that hung in the air. I had the sense that Franc wanted to tell Marcos to shove it, but didn't want to speak for Caden either.

"Fine, Marcos, have it your way." Caden sighed, his shoulders slumping forward. "The seeds aren't just old or a family relic, they're the last magical remnants of the original huppulu tree," Caden explained. "They belong to my Granny Lily, who will probably skin me alive when she discovers they're gone."

Caden didn't look like he was joking. How important were these seeds?

"Is that a metaphorical or literal skinning?" I asked.

The look he gave me confirmed the latter. I shuddered. We needed more than plans A through C if the situation were that dire.

"Why would your old Granny kill you over seeds? Are they for growing a beanstalk into another realm?"

When Caden replied, his voice was low. "No. When the huppulu grows again, Granny will carve a throne out of it to rule from."

"Rule what?" Liam asked, his brow creased in a way I was beginning to consider dashing. "The Netherworld?"

Caden shook his head. "No. Everything."

There was a moment of silence all around, and I suspected I wasn't the only one trying to figure out if Caden was joking.

Marcos burst into laughter, breaking our silence. "And you stole granny's sacred pearls? You got a death wish?"

Caden raked a hand through his hair, the anxiety he'd been trying to play off this quest finally rising to the surface. "It seemed like a low-risk proposition at the time. I could show off a family legacy with no one missing it for a couple of days. I hadn't counted on us being manipulated by the fae or going on this joyride into hell."

"Hey, at least if Granny doesn't kill you, you can fall

back on your drug trade and partying it up with lowlifes," Marcos said.

Franc and Liam jumped to their feet, wedging themselves between Marcos and Caden, deflecting Caden's right hook just in time.

"I'm going to ask you both to sit down and take a few deep breaths," Franc said.

"Not gonna happen, Franc," Caden snapped back. There was an intensity in his gaze I hadn't seen before. A resolute clarity. "Look, I'm done taking your crap and being talked down to, Marcos. I'm not what you think. I've been working for the Supe branch of the Drug Enforcement Agency."

Caden was a narc? From the look on Liam's face, Marcos wasn't the only one this was news to. As I thought about it, it explained a lot of the disconnect between Caden's bad boy reputation and the controlled, thoughtful person I'd spent time around these past few days.

Marcos took a couple of unsteady steps back, his face screwed up with disbelief. "That doesn't make any sense. You barely got enough credits to finish the academy and I'm supposed to believe you're with the Supe Feds?"

"Right? What else would you expect from a lust-drunk demon besides sex, drugs, and parties?" Caden spat out.

Franc cleared his throat. "It's true, Marcos. Caden's been working leads out of Velvet with my blessing the past two years now."

Marcos' jaw dropped open. "You knew? I mean, yeah, of course you knew what the demon was up to." He planted his hands on his hips. "I don't know what's worse. Thinking you're a drug dealer or knowing neither of you trusted me enough to bring me into your confidence."

"It wasn't like that, Marcos," Franc said. "We didn't want to put you in a dangerous position."

"No, instead you used me. Both of you did."

If Caden and Marcos kept going at it, soon the proverbial fur would be flying. I took Marcos by the hand, pulling him away from Caden and toward a bedroom. "Enough talk. We all need some sleep if we're going to be up early in the morning." The panther shifter dug in his heels, his lip raised like a snarl, like he was about to attack. I got up in his face and appealed to an altogether different animal nature. "Can I trust you to watch over me while I sleep, or do I need to ask someone else?"

Marcos' snarl disappeared, replaced by shock. "Of course you can trust me."

I threaded my fingers around his arm, loving his boxer-like build, and drug him along to the bedroom. Marcos could have resisted, but I'd bet on his protective shifter instincts kicking in. When we got to the door, I looked back at the others, and for a moment, I wanted the safety of all of them cuddled up against me. I shook my head. That could wait. Right now, Marcos needed me.

Franc and Caden were walking, not noticing my furtive glance, but Liam was watching me. He arched a brow, as if asking if I wanted more company. I shook my head, and the wolf gave a single nod. I closed the door behind Marcos and myself and got ready for bed.

Marcos watched me change and pull my hair up into a ponytail, his eyes full of questions as he sat down on one bed in the simple room.

I planted myself next to him, leaning into his space. "Whatever it is, just say it."

"I'm just hurt, okay?" he said in a low voice.

"Tell me more?"

"All this time I've been hating Caden, thinking the worst of him really, and it turns out it was all an act? I'm upset they didn't trust me to know the truth, and upset he and Franc let me carry on being awful to him for years just to keep up this show."

I slid an arm around Marcos, my heart echoing the pain in his words.

"That's a lot of lost time," I said. "But you know now, so the healing can start."

He shook his head. "We used to be so close. All of that slipped away while Caden played this role." Marcos scrubbed a hand over his head. "I get he believes in his cause, but it's going to take me some time to process."

"I suspect he'll give you all the time you need. Why don't we get some sleep? I hear morning comes at o'dark thirty." I smiled, hoping he'd let the conflict go, at least for the night.

He smiled back, but it was half-hearted. "A night alone with you? I'd never pass that up."

I bit my lip. "You're not bothered over missing out on the shower earlier?"

Marcos reached out and tucked a loose strand of hair behind my ear. "I'd prefer to never leave your side, but you're a grown ass woman, Sera. I won't tell you who to be with, or when. I just count myself lucky that I'm here with you now."

My heart melted over his words, and I leaned in for a kiss that did not disappoint. He pulled back and undressed, throwing his clothes on the chair and then pulled the covers back and laid down on the bed. A mottled pattern of red and black bruising covered his shin and calf, no doubt from the wraiths in the river earlier.

"That looks like it hurts," I said. "Now I feel even worse about knocking you off that raft."

"Don't trouble yourself, Sera. It looks worse than it feels," he replied. "Now come over here and let me warm you up."

I curled up next to him, spooning up against his warmth as he wrapped one of those big, muscular arms around me.

I might be in the Netherworld, but somehow surrounded by Marcos and the others, I'd never felt safer. I drifted off to a deep, dreamless sleep, only to awaken a few hours later. My brain was in overdrive, knowing I'd have to get up soon and didn't want to oversleep.

I snuggled up against Marcos, the heat of his body drawing me like a moth to the flame. When he pulled me tight against him, his erection pressed against my ass, all worries about trudging uphill in the dark and sneaking up on a winged monster fled my mind. I'd already tasted that beautiful cock of his once, and now I wanted more.

I ground my hips back against him, deliberately teasing for a reaction. "Are you awake?" I asked, my voice a whisper.

The deep-throated sound Marcos made deep in this throat was almost a purr. "You can bet I am now." His hand slipped under my shirt, cupping my breast in his hand, before he found and rolled my nipple between his fingers. I let out a low groan, loving the attention.

"What do you say we blow off some steam before we get up?" I tried to roll over and face him, but Marcos shifted his weight, pinning my legs in place with his hips while he continued to tease my nipple between his fingers. Heat bloomed between my legs, and I writhed against Marcos, craving more skin on skin contact. What had started off as a flirtation had quickly transformed into a demand.

He tugged at the hem of my shirt, and I pulled it off over my head. Marcos rewarded me with a line of kisses down my neck, nuzzling as he went. "Is that all this is? Blowing off steam?"

Was it just about the stress, or something more? I searched my heart, then my gut, and realized I didn't want to think too hard about it. "It's complicated how I feel about you and the posse. Can't it be fun, and maybe something more too?"

Saying those words, the possibility of something more hit me right in the gut. I enjoyed being around them and loved the sex and developing friendships. But when I thought about more, I had to think of what might happen after the quest for the posse's stolen legacies. What might work now, in this faery-created bubble, didn't translate well to the normal world.

"There's no maybe for me, Sera," he said, the timbre of his voice low and rumbling against the skin of my shoulder. He pulled away, hooking his thumbs around the waistband of my sweatpants. He bit the skin of my hip, gently but in a proprietary way. "Is this what you want?" he asked, tugging at my pants.

"Yesss," I said, hissing the word.

"Stay right there," he growled. Marcos pulled my sweatpants and panties off. I heard the tearing of a condom wrapper, and then Marcos' weight was back on top of me as he kissed and nibbled his way up my back.

But just when I felt his erection press against my core, he paused.

Marcos traced a finger over my shoulders, over the marks I still hadn't gotten a good look at. "I wish there were better mirrors here, then you could see what I see."

"Enough about those marks," I said, squirming against him, trying to get him inside of me, but he had me pinned into the position he wanted. Dominant much, Marcos? "We have more pressing concerns, lover."

He chuckled, and then kissed where my shoulder met my neck. "I want to be inside you, almost as much as I want to claim you as my own." He rolled his hips, sliding against me.

"Wait, I thought you said your mark was already on me? And stop teasing me, kitty, scratch that itch!"

He chuckled, but then relented, driving his cock deep into me. I gasped, loving the feel of him inside of me, his musky scent filling my nostrils.

"This mark shows you're fated to be mine, but there's also the claiming mark."

I had a general sense of how shifters mated, but being a mage, I hadn't overly concerned myself with the mechanics. "Remind me how that works? I'm kind of distracted."

"Kind of?" he muttered, then upped his pacing. "Let me see what I can do about that." He then leaned in and bit my neck oh so gently.

A lightning of sensation spread over my flesh emanating from where his teeth met my skin. I thrashed under him as the sensation grew and grew. My body responded with an orgasm so intense, I saw black, and then stars, and then brilliant colors. A moment later, Marcos came, still gripping my flesh in his teeth.

When we'd both caught our breath, he pulled back and rolled off me. "I'll bite you like that, except I'll break the skin. Oh my gods, was that hard to hold back just now."

I certainly most definitely wanted more Marcos. But mates? "I don't know if I'll want that, Marcos."

"I understand. It's a lot, and it's not just my mark on your back either. It's a lot to process."

I sighed, running my fingers through my hair. "We don't know if those marks appeared just because we went through the faery portal together. They might just be some fae trick, too. After we're done with this quest, all of those marks might disappear."

"Sure, we can't know for sure. But what if they are?"

"Then I'll deal with it then, Marcos. Right now we're not in the real world, so we have to make the best of what we've got."

"Not the real world?" he said, and by his gruff tone, I knew I'd gotten his hackles up. "What makes things real, Sera? I mean, if we decide it's real, doesn't that make it real?"

I rolled over onto him, pulling him into a slow, wet, kiss. "You're such a romantic, kitty."

"I suppose I am." Marcos ran a hand down my side, the motion feeling so familiar and comforting. "I could go for another round," he whispered, planting a kiss on my forehead, "but I'm sure the others are expecting us."

I could so easily have fallen back asleep beside Marcos. I felt so safe and cherished when I was with him, but I knew he was right that we were tight on time. I pushed myself up, looking around for my clothes. "Oh yeah, another fun day in faery retaliation land awaits us."

"You had an out, yet you chose to stay."

It wasn't a question, yet it was. "I couldn't go. Emrys called in his boon for me to help negotiate things with Taneisha. It's not his fault this has led into a multi-day journey." I found my jeans, pulling them up as I stood up.

"So you're staying just for Emrys?" he asked, a pained look in his eyes as he watched me dress.

I leaned in close, giving him a quick kiss on the tip of his nose. "No, I won't leave any of you with her, not if I can help it."

Marcos raised his brows, a gleam of triumph in his eyes. "That's a little proprietary of you, mage. I like it."

I pulled my shirt over my head and then turned to him. "I don't know about this fated mates thing, but I definitely feel protective of my posse." He grinned at my admission. "Now get a move on, kitty. We've got a legacy to recover."

RING OF FIRE

CADEN

When Marcos and Sera emerged from their room, I had absolutely no question in my mind what had delayed them. Sera's hair was mussed, a flush filled her cheeks, and her lips were plump and swollen. Their aura was a lovely shade of rose gold, and for once in a long while, Marcos didn't look like he was on the verge of pouncing and biting anyone's head off.

Thank the gods for small mercies.

"Did we slow everyone down?" Sera asked, catching her breath as she pulled her backpack up over her shoulders.

"Not at all," Liam replied. "Everyone ready to go?"

I envied the wolf, who seemed to take the integration of Sera into our ranks with ease. As each day progressed, the mage was less our 'fae mediator' and more our companion, which I wasn't entirely sure how to feel about. Were those marks covering her shoulders truly mating marks, revealing a soul bond between all of us?

I'd placed myself firmly within the 'wait and see' camp. Or maybe the 'keep calm and fuck on' camp. Based on Liam, Marcos, and Franc's eagerness to bed Sera, I had a pretty clear notion of how they felt having her along for the, uh, ride, as it were.

But what would happen after we completed Taneisha's quests? Would we go back to our lives as they were, pretending none of this had happened? The idea sent a wave of uneasiness rolling over me. Wait. What the hell? Did I want this temporary arrangement to continue?

"Caden, are you ready?" Sera asked.

Everyone was looking at me, and here I was staring off into the aether like a loon. I gave myself a shake. I had to stay in the game if we were going to get the upper hand on the Anzu.

"Yeah, I'm fine. Just psyching myself up for the fight."

Franc placed a reassuring hand on my shoulder. "Hopefully, per your plan, we can avoid the actual fight."

"Let's move," Marcos said.

We closed up the hunting cabin, leaving it pretty much exactly as we'd found it, except for some used sheets and towels. Franc had left a couple of twenties on top of the pile for whomever had to handle the laundry later.

I led the way back to the trail in the dim light of pre-dawn, my thoughts warring between focusing on landmarks from the map and memories of my time in the shower with Franc and Sera. As fun as it had been, images of having her, or them, again, filled my thoughts.

"How's your magic today?" Franc asked Sera.

I glanced back at them, wary of Franc's line of questioning after his intensity yesterday.

Sera arched her brow. "What, you worried I'm gonna go supernova?"

Franc held a hand to his chest, feigning shock. "Is that even an option? Now I'm kind of curious, actually."

"Sera's already gone supernova," I quipped before I could catch my tongue.

"What, no!" she exclaimed, eyes wide. "I haven't set anything on fire. Not lately."

"Didn't you refer to our posse as the Supernova of Hotness a couple of days ago?" I said, unable to keep the joke inside my own damned head. "Seems to me you're getting quite a handle on our supernova." Now that I'd said them, my words sounded harsher than I'd meant.

"Uh," she stammered, cheeks flushing a lovely shade of rose, but she recovered quickly, barking out a laugh. "I suppose you've got me there. Nice detective work, officer. But, to answer Franc's question, my magic feels pretty stable. It's a pleasant change."

"Perhaps your powers just require a regular and liberal application of supernova hotness?" Franc asked.

Damn, how I loved Franc's humor. Sera snickered at his suggestion, but I had to wonder. Was there any truth to it?

A screeching cry rang out in the distance, squashing our conversation. Part squawk, part roar, and one hundred percent intimidating. The sound echoed down the valley our trail led through. We instinctively bunched up together, huddling close, as if the beast was already right on top of us.

"That sounded... bigger than expected," Liam whispered. Neither he nor Marcos looked afraid. I hoped I looked as sure of myself as they did, but doubted it.

"That's what she said," Sera murmured. All heads turned to the mage, who at least had the grace to shrug. "Sorry. Sarcasm is my crutch."

We waited in silence for something to happen. There was a second screech. Then a third. After that, the mountain felt eerily quiet, as if all other resident creatures feared the one who'd uttered that call.

After a few minutes passed in silence, despite my every instinct to get away from the Anzu, I forged ahead on the trail, headed straight toward the monster.

Franc caught up with me, walking quietly beside me for a few moments. When he spoke, it was in a whisper. "You sure about this?"

I nodded. "I have to get those seeds back. I won't let them fall into the wrong hands."

"That's tough when the right hands are also not so great," Franc said. "I don't envy your situation with your Granny."

The ground underfoot grew steep and uneven, but luckily the dawn was near, making it possible to continue threading our way through the scrub brush and thorny thickets dotting the landscape.

A rush of wings passed by overhead. Panicking, I ducked, doing my best to imitate a nearby bush. Looking back, I saw the others had done the same. Soon enough, the creature had moved on. I waited a moment, maybe two, and then rushed toward the direction it had come from, guessing its nest had to be close by. I scrambled up a rise of small boulders, hearing the others behind me follow. When I crested the mound, I saw what had to be the monster's nest spread out within the hollow below.

It was huge, reminding me of a large, sprawling eagle's

nest, except it was twenty times the size. I pulled a flashlight from my pocket and turned it on, keeping the beam low. Marcos and Franc followed suit.

When I looked around and noticed Liam had shifted into his wolf form, it let me know how focused I'd become that I'd missed his change. He darted back and forth through the jumble of sticks and twigs, nosing about faster than the rest of us.

"Ew," Sera said, her voice a whisper as she poked at a small pile of bones and fur with the toe of her shoe. "This nest is filthy." She turned to me. "What do the seeds look like?"

"I forget you didn't see it at the party," I laughed. Of course she hadn't, but after the past couple of days, it seemed like Sera had become a fixture. "They're in a small clay jar that's glazed a dark purple. If it's still in one piece, it'll stand out," I explained.

Another minute of frantic searching passed before Liam let out a short yip. He scratched at a tangle of feathers and then sat down next to it.

Sera was right there, pulling branches out of the way before extracting the purple jar I knew by shape alone. "This it?"

I rushed to them, taking the jar from her outstretched hands. "Yes!" I exclaimed. I shook the jar, hearing the telltale rattle of the seeds inside it. Then I opened it, pouring the contents out into my hand. The seeds were black as night, so potent and powerful I could feel waves of demonic energy pouring off of them. I quickly shoved the seeds back inside and sealed the lid tight. "Oh yeah, it's them."

"Wait, will Taneisha consider this stealing?" Sera

asked.

"She said the Anzu stole from her, so I hope turnabout is fair play?"

"We'll have to hope." Franc clapped me on the shoulder. "Then let's get out of here before it gets back."

There's a magic to summoning trouble, and the key element is always that full-body feeling of relief when the finish line is in sight. Which is why I wasn't surprised when the sound of wings barreling toward us, followed by an angry screech, rang out overhead.

"Shit," Franc yelled.

The Anzu appeared with a sudden thwack as its full weight at speed hit the nest; the impact causing the wood beneath his clawed feet to crack and shatter. He was naked except for the coating of dark grey feathers covering his body and massive wings. His arms ended in clawed talons, matching his feet. His beaked face was hard to read, but I assumed the glow of crimson in his eyes meant he wasn't happy to see us.

Liam's hackles rose, a low growl emanating from his throat. I knew he was ready and willing to fight, but I couldn't let that happen.

"Sera! Fire?" I said, falling back on my eloquent nature. I pointed to the ground in an arc between us and the Anzu.

I knew it was a risk. Sera had explained her magic wasn't always stable, but we needed something to prevent the monster from biting our heads off.

Sera stepped up beside me, holding her hands out as her face twisted in concentration while the Anzu advanced on us, his wings wide and talons at the ready. Fear shot through me, as I realized I'd placed Sera head to head with the monster. I thought to pull her back or place myself between them, but then all at once, mage fire poured from her fingertips, lighting the nest on fire between us and the Anzu.

As the purplish-pink flames leapt into the air and the monster shrieked and glowered, I got us out of here. "Taneisha, Taneisha, Taneisha," I called out, hoping she'd come when called like the last time, even if we were mid-battle with an ancient monster.

A whoosh of air behind us was followed by a peal of laughter that echoed over the mountainside. I glanced back to see Taneisha standing before her portal, shaking her head as she clapped. She stood resplendent, in a dress made seemingly from the starry night sky and her blonde pulled back into a long, single braid.

"Didn't I say to call for me when you finished your quest?" she asked. "Looks like you're still wrapping this one up."

I grabbed Sera's arm with my free hand, encouraging her to run towards the portal with me. I held the jar up, showing her the evidence of our success. "Got it right here!"

"Great!" Taneisha flashed me a thumb's up, but then crossed her arms. "So what's the holdup?"

I ground my teeth. At least she wasn't leaving, but it was clear the fae wouldn't help us, either. Franc and Marcos, who'd been further from the Anzu, made it back to the portal first. Liam bounded along behind them, with Sera and I taking up the rear.

The Anzu let out a piercing caw. He leapt into the air, and for the briefest of moments I thought he fled, but then a blast of air in my face brought Sera and I to a standstill as the Anzu landed in front of us, blocking our path to the portal. "Those are not yours to take," he said, eyeing the jar in my hand.

I pulled Sera close to my side. We were cut off from the others and the portal, our only way to escape this literal hellhole. I watched as Franc held Marcos back, while an irate and very naked Liam argued with a seemingly unconcerned Taneisha.

"Did you have a plan D?" Sera asked.

"Sure I do." Of course I did, but I hated that we'd reached this juncture almost out of the gate. "These are mine," I yelled at the Anzu, figuring perhaps I could still talk my way out of this.

The bird-man threw back his head, laughing up into the grey dawn sky of the Netherworld, before returning his attention to the jar of seeds I held in my hand. "Those are not yours, incubus. Lilith is their rightful owner. Leave them, and I will let you live."

"Your Granny Lily is the Lilith?" Sera asked, eyes wide with recognition. "You call her Granny?"

"Yeah. Family gets complicated, you know?"

Sera shot me a wry smile. "Truer words..."

How did the creature know the history of the seeds? Was it reading my mind or magically gifted in recognizing items? Whichever, I supposed it didn't matter. It had me dead to rights. "Lilith is my grandmother. I borrowed the huppulu seeds from her and I need to return them."

"Then why don't I believe you, wretch?" the Anzu said, advancing a step towards them. "Why would you steal them, knowing how precious they are to our queen?"

That's precisely why, although I wouldn't admit it to the beast. Sure, Franc's legacy challenge had given me an excuse, but my fear of Lily's plans to use the seeds to bring a rebirth of demonic power on earth had driven my choice. Only now, facing the beast, could I accept the truth.

I'd never planned to return the seeds.

The Anzu took another step forward. "Give them to me, and I'll make sure they end up safe where they belong."

I knew if I resisted, the Anzu would tear me apart to get the seeds back. I couldn't endanger Sera because of my impulsive behavior, nor could I allow my grandmother to have the seeds back.

"Fine," I said. "Here, have them!" I pivoted and threw the jar into the line of mage fire burning brightly behind us, hearing the jar rupture on impact.

The Anzu shrieked, bounding into the air above us as we ducked, intent on flying into harm's way to salvage the seeds. As soon as the monster was behind us, I grabbed Sera by the hand and raced toward the portal. There was a blast as a series of punctuated explosions cracked through the air like a massive firecracker.

So much for taking over the world, Granny.

Only when we reached the portal did we stop and look back. The Anzu stood bereft, holding ashes in his great taloned hands. Scorch marks covered his feathers. "Our queen will know what you've done, incubus. I will make sure of it."

I tried to ignore the sinking feeling in my gut. This wasn't something I could take back. There would be consequences, but I'd worry about those on another day. Now I was just glad to be alive.

I nodded to the Anzu, and then turned and walked through the portal with my family of choice by my side.

EPILOGUE: EMRYS AWAKENED

SERA

Returning to Taneisha's faery glen felt like a welcome measure of safety, but only compared to the facing off against actual hellions. The posse looked like they'd been through hell because they had. Everyone was catching their breath, tossing their backpacks to the ground, and checking themselves over.

Marcos ran to me and scooped me up into his arms, his embrace crushingly tight. "Don't you ever do that again, little mage." He shuddered as he took a deep breath, his nose buried in my hair.

His desire to keep me safe was endearing. "I'm okay, Marcos, really. We're all okay, thanks to Caden's sacrifice."

Marcos pulled away from me, only to have Liam draw me into his arms next.

"I don't know what I'd do if we lost you," he whispered in my ear.

I hugged Liam back, my palms sliding along the bare skin of his back. "But you didn't, and I'm not going anywhere. But you can put some clothes on now that we're out of danger." He chuckled, but then did just that.

Taneisha strode back through the portal, closing it after herself and cutting off the lamentations of the Anzu in the Netherworld. She sauntered over to a throne-like chair, her gown of stars trailing behind her as if she were in some sort of fashion show.

Marcos walked up to Caden and held his hand out. "I misjudged you, brother. What you did today? What you've been doing for your job undercover? You're a stronger man than I ever realized. If I were in your shoes, I don't think I'd have been able to persevere."

A look of sorrow passed over Caden's face. I wondered if he was thinking about how working undercover had damaged his relationships? At least now they had an opportunity to reset and move forward.

He took Marcos' hand and then pulled the panther shifter in for a hug. "It's okay. I didn't exactly give you a reason to think better of me. I'm sorry I left you in the dark."

Marcos chuckled. "I get it, man. Now that I'm in the know, I'm happy to help play the game with you."

I stepped up to Caden, threw my arms around his neck, and planted a kiss on his cheek. "Good job, you sexy demon you."

"Look, I think I speak for all of us when I say how damned proud we are of you. But how are you going to handle your grandmother?" Franc asked Caden. "She's gonna lose her shit when she finds out."

Caden shrugged. "Well, I can't take it back now. The Anzu will tell Lily what happened, so I suppose I'll deal with her temper when I have to. I don't regret destroying the seeds and ruining her plans. It was the right thing to do."

Taneisha cleared her throat, and we all quieted, turning our anxious attention toward the troublesome fae. Oh yeah, we were one more legacy down, but we still had three more to go.

Having regained our attention, she smiled sweetly. "If you're done post-almost-dying-bonding, I'd love to introduce you to the next challenge?"

Franc marched up to her throne. "Where's Emrys?"

Taneisha held up a finger, cautioning him. "In a moment, wine god." She snapped her fingers, and the tree portal opened again. This time it was sunny on the other side with a view of a tall, neatly trimmed hedge row leading off into the distance. "I've hidden the wolf's heart within the center of this maze. Just as love is a maze, full of twists and turns, so is this puzzle. You have three days to find your icon, Liam, or lose it to fate, forever."

Liam, who'd dressed again, looked wary. And why wouldn't he? "How big is a maze that takes three days to solve?"

Taneisha pursed her lips, and then leaned in, as if about to share some juicy secret with us. "It's not about size, silly. This one is all skill. Also, the rules from round one apply again. No cheating. No stealing. One three-day shot."

"Sounds easier than hell," I replied. "What's your twist?"

The fae held her hands up, doing her best wide-eyed impression of an innocent person. "What do you mean? You know what a maze is. This is pretty straightforward for a challenge, to be honest."

I remembered several mazes from the history books at the academy. "From what I recall, most mazes have traps, illusions, and the occasional monster?"

"See, I knew you knew. Like I said, it's totally standard."

Great. Hopefully, we wouldn't run into any minotaurs along the way. From looking around at the guys' grim and frowning faces, I could tell I wasn't the only one worried.

"I've gone to the liberty of prepping some new travel bags for you. And oh yes, your missing companion!" Taneisha snapped her fingers again, and Emrys appeared out of thin air, curled up in a ball at her feet. "He really has missed you, but as you can see, he's fine."

Emrys shuddered, taking deep breaths. Like hells, he was fine!

"What did you do to him?" Franc demanded.

"He was in a sensory deprivation chamber, getting some good quality time with himself." She smiled, but the fae's eyes seethed with a vindictive glare. "Now it's free and ready for the next member of the posse who violates the rules of the game."

"Wait, he's been in there the whole time?" I asked, and her smile widened. "But that's been days." I wasn't an expert, but I knew that long periods in sensory deprivation could drive a person mad. How had Emrys kept it together?

Emrys bolted upright, a wild look in his eyes. He looked around, taking us all in, but I had the impression he was still in something of an altered state. His clothes looked rumpled, like he'd been in them for days, which he likely had. I swore to myself. This was beyond the pale, even for the aggrieved fae.

Caden crouched low, getting down on Emrys' level. Liam did the same. I hung back with Marcos, not wanting to overwhelm him. Franc looked so pissed, I expected him to explode at any second.

"Hey man, it's good to see you're all right," Caden said, his voice oozing calm.

"I know you're not Caden," Emrys said, his voice hoarse, as if he'd been screaming. He turned to Liam. "Not really. And you're not the wolf." He looked around at each of us. "I know better now. None of you can fool me anymore."

Yeah... Emrys hadn't kept it together. Oh boy.

We exchanged glances, no one appearing sure what to say or do to reassure the addled demi-god. In that pause, Emrys shot to his feet and bolted, slipping his way between Liam and Caden and making it through the portal before any of us could react.

"That could have gone better," Franc snapped. "Let's get a move on. We can't let him get too much of a head start." He turned, grabbed two of the backpacks, and he rushed off after Emrys. Caden and Liam grabbed the old and new backpacks, and then were hot on Franc's heels, while Marcos waited at the portal for me carrying both of our backpacks.

I sighed, turning back toward Taneisha. "I'm grateful Emrys is still alive, but seriously, are you trying to kill us?"

The fae had the grace to look shocked. "Oh, of course I don't want you dead, dearest." She blew me a kiss. "The rest of them, however..." she trailed off, leaving me to fear the worst.

I could have shrugged it off, but I needed to leverage

what little I had. "Taneisha, if you allow the posse to die, know you'll have made an enemy of the Lowe's."

Taneisha rolled her eyes. "What do I care if some mages dislike me?"

I moved closer to her, staring her down. "Not just any mages. The Lowe lineage is one of, if not the, most powerful mages around. You sure you and your family want a war with ours?"

I didn't know if the rest of the Lowes would back me up on this, but mages were known for their wars between houses which sometimes lasted for decades.

Taneisha's ever present smug smile stiffened. "War over a game? Of course not. How about this? If anyone gets hurt, have them call me and I'll pull them out of this round and give them a healing elixir. They won't be able to return to the maze and help find the wolf's heart, and your team will be down one, but they won't die. How's that?"

"It's acceptable. Thank you."

Her over the top smile was back. "Better get going. You don't want to miss any of the fun."

I walked through the portal, Marcos at my side, pretty certain Taneisha and I did not share the same definition of fun.

THE END

Thank you so much for reading Entangled Essence! It would mean a lot to me if you could leave a review. A single line or two makes a big difference for other people when deciding if a book is a good fit for them.

The next book in the series, Hidden Hearts, is available for preorder now.

The quest for Caden's legacy might not have gone to plan, but at least the Supernova of Hotness has Emrys back with the pack. Well, most of him. Can Sera and the posse navigate the treacherous living maze and find Liam's legacy while helping Emrys regain his brittle sanity?

ALSO BY CANDICE BUNDY

The Stolen Legacy Series

Forbidden Fates

Entangled Essence

Hidden Hearts

The Shadow Series

Shadow in the City, A prequel novella

Twinned Shadow

Poisoned Shadow

Shadow Underground

Caught Between Worlds Series

Smoke and Daemons

(previously published as Daemon Whisperer)

Other Works

Ripples, a novella

Open Rack, a contemporary short

WRITING AS CR BUNDY

The Depths of Memory Series

The Dream Sifter

Dreams Manifest

For a list of my full catalog of available titles, visit my <u>Amazon Author Central</u> page.

ALSO BY PIPER FOX

Academy for Reapers: Paranormal Romance

Big Wolf on Campus Series: Wolf Shifter Football Romances

The Stolen Legacy Series: Paranormal Reverse Harem

Midnight Huntress Series: Paranormal Reverse Harem

Alien Warriors of New Dilaria Series: Sci-Fi Reverse Harem

The Ironhaven Pack Series: Wolf Shifter Romances

The Dragon Space Order Bride Series: Sci-Fi Romance

<u>Bears of Crooked Creek</u>: A Bear Shifter Romance Series

<u>Seven Brides For Seven Demons</u>: A Demon Romance Series

<u>Last Warriors of Dilaria</u>: A Sci-Fi Romance Series

The Immortal Blood Series: Vampire Romance

ABOUT CANDICE BUNDY

Candice lives in Denver, Colorado with her son and their cat Newt. A professional hedonist, rabble-rouser, winemaker, and goat-herder, she adores archeology and mythology. Candice focuses on habit hacking to meet minimalist, health, productivity, and positive mojo goals, and sometimes even blogs about it. An unrepentant epicurean, she grows heirloom tomatoes and ferments a variety of sauerkraut, sourdough, kombucha, pickles, and water kefir.

If you would like to know when she has new books out, please sign up for her newsletter here. Email her if the mood strikes you.

For more information:
candicebundy.com
candice@candicebundy.com

ABOUT PIPER FOX

Piper Fox writes steamy paranormal romances for sassy, strong-willed women and the sexy, alpha men who love them.

Follow her on:
Facebook: facebook.com/PiperFoxAuthor
Bookbub: https://www.bookbub.com/profile/piper-fox